'Good idea?' he asked, his eyes indicating the glass London Eye capsule they were in. 'Do you think the boys are enjoying it?'

Jemima couldn't believe he was experiencing a moment of doubt about it, but his blue eyes seemed to be waiting for an answer. 'It's brilliant. They're loving it. Thank you.'

Then he smiled, and she wondered whether it was doing her heart any permanent damage to keep beating so erratically. For thirty years she hadn't experienced the slightest difficulty, but since meeting Miles it had been behaving very peculiarly.

'Are you?'

She nodded, feeling unaccountably shy.

'Come see,' he said, holding out his hand.

Slowly, her heart pounding, Jemima put her hand inside his. She'd seen a movie once where they'd talked about looking down and not knowing where one hand left off and the other began. It felt a little like that, except that she knew which hand belonged to whom. His hand was dark against her fair skin. It was more that she felt as if it belonged there.

*TenderRomance™ is thrilled to bring you another
sparkling new book from British author*

Natasha Oakley

*Her poignant and emotional writing
will tug on your heartstrings.*

'Her words shoot straight to your heart just like cupid's
arrow. Ms Oakley has a special talent for making you
fall in love with her characters.'
—*writersunlimited.com*

'One of the best writers of
contemporary romance writing today!'
—*cataromance.com*

'Emotional, romantic and unforgettable,
Natasha Oakley aims straight for your heart
with richly drawn characters, powerfully intense
emotions and heartstopping romance!'
—*cataromance.com*

ACCEPTING THE BOSS'S PROPOSAL

BY
NATASHA OAKLEY

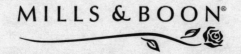

MILLS & BOON®

First published in Great Britain 2006
by Harlequin Mills & Boon Limited,
Eton House, 18-24 Paradise Road, Richmond, Surrey TW9 1SR

© Natasha Oakley 2006

Standard ISBN: 0 263 84922 8
Promotional ISBN: 0 263 85478 7

Set in Times Roman 12 on 14 pt.
02-0906-54480

Printed and bound in Spain
by Litografia Rosés S.A., Barcelona

Natasha Oakley told everyone at her primary school that she wanted to be an author when she grew up. Her plan was to stay at home and have her mum bring her coffee at regular intervals—a drink she didn't like then. The coffee addiction became reality, and the love of storytelling stayed with her. A professional actress, Natasha began writing when her fifth child started to sleep through the night. Born in London, she now lives in Bedfordshire with her husband and young family. When not writing, or needed for 'crowd control', she loves to escape to antiques fairs and auctions. Find out more about Natasha and her books on her website www.natashaoakley.com

Recent titles by the same author:

MILLIONAIRE DAD: WIFE NEEDED
ORDINARY GIRL, SOCIETY GROOM
A FAMILY TO BELONG TO
  Heart to Heart
THE BUSINESS ARRANGEMENT

CHAPTER ONE

SHE'D made a mistake.

Jemima knew it the minute she saw what the woman on the reception desk was wearing. Kingsley and Bressington might sound like some staid turn-of-the-last-century law firm, but the reality was completely different—and the woman on the reception desk embodied exactly that.

She wore a rich brown T-shirt which hugged the kind of yoga-toned body that always made Jemima feel vaguely depressed. Dramatic turquoise jewellery picked out an exact shade in the receptionist's vibrant skirt and brought out the colour of her eyes. Her look was overwhelmingly young…fashionable…and a world away from Jemima's borrowed suit. Its aubergine colour might be perfect with her carefully straightened red hair, but it was entirely too formal for Kingsley and Bressington.

Nor was she quite sure how she could dress any differently tomorrow. Even if her own wardrobe wasn't restricted to jeans and easy care fabrics, she was two children too late for that kind of body conscious clothing.

Jemima glanced around the acres of white walls, taking in the abstract paintings and sculptural plants in huge stainless steel pots. What the heck was she doing in a trendy place like this? If she didn't know she'd be letting Amanda down she'd turn tail and run now. Fast. This wasn't what she'd wanted at all.

Instead she made herself stand firm. She could hardly balk at her first placement and this was about so much more than one temporary job. This was about standing on her own feet, recovering her self-esteem, making a new beginning... All those trite phrases that everyone instinctively churned out when they were confronted by the rejected half of a 'now divorced' couple.

That she believed they were right was probably something to do with the British 'stiff upper lip' thing that was buried deep in her psyche. She twisted the gold chain at her neck. God forbid she should break down and cry. Or curl under her duvet and refuse to emerge until the world had settled back to the way it had been before. She had to be strong. For the boys. Everyone said so...

Jemima took a shaky breath and waited for the receptionist to finish her telephone call. She'd already been cast an apologetic 'I'll be with you in a moment' look and watched with growing fatalism as the receptionist tapped her acrylic-tipped nails impatiently on the glass table while she explained why she couldn't transfer the caller to the person they wanted.

She could do this. She *could*. Jemima made herself stand a little straighter and concentrated on exuding confidence. What was it Amanda had said about 'transferable skills'? All those years of PTA involvement had to amount to something. Not to mention her degree, secretarial qualifications…

'I'm so sorry to have kept you waiting. Can I help you?'

Jemima jerked to attention, a small part of her mind still free to speculate on whether the receptionist's long hair was the result of nature…or extensions. 'Jemima Chadwick. I'm Jemima Chadwick. From Harper Recruitment. I'm here to temp for Miles Kingsley and I'm to ask for…' She pulled her handbag off her shoulder and started to rummage through Visa slips and assorted pieces of screwed-up paper. Somewhere in the depths of her bag was the small notebook in which she'd written all the details Amanda had given her on Friday afternoon.

Somewhere…

'Saskia Longthorne,' the receptionist said with authority. 'She deals with all temporary staff. I'll let her know you're here.'

Too late. Just too late Jemima pulled the piece of paper out of her bag and looked down at the words she'd scribbled.

'She won't keep you a moment. If you'd like to take a seat?' There was the faintest trace of a question in her modulated voice, but Jemima had no difficulty in recognising a directive.

She balled the piece of paper up in her hand. 'Th-thank you.'

Jemima turned and went to sit on one of the seats. They were set in a semi-circular format around an unusual shattered glass coffee table and were the kind of low-slung design that required the same impossible skills as climbing in and out of a sports car. She perched uncomfortably on the edge in a vain effort to stop her skirt from riding up.

This morning she'd been hyped up for the challenge of rebuilding her life. A new beginning—and this temporary job was merely the first step. But now she was actually here…all that beautiful confidence was evaporating. Everything about Kingsley and Bressington made her feel uncomfortable. It was all so far outside of her personal experience it hurt.

But then, that was the idea. Amanda had been adamant that she ought to test her new skills in several temporary vacancies before she looked for a permanent position. She should see what kind of working environment she preferred, push the boundaries a little… As Amanda had said, she might surprise herself with the choices she'd make.

At least, that had been the theory. Sitting in Amanda Symmond's comfortable Oxford Street offices, it had seemed like a very good idea, but right now she'd give up practically everything to be at home and loading her boys into the back of her Volvo for the school run. Safe. Doing what she knew.

As the minutes slipped by, Jemima sank back into her seat and stopped jumping at the sound of every footstep.

'Jemima Chadwick? Mrs Chadwick?'

She looked up at the sound of a masculine voice. 'Yes. That's me. I…' She struggled to pull herself out of the deep seat while still clutching her handbag. 'I'm sorry…I was told to wait here for Saskia Longthorne,' she managed foolishly, looking up into a pair of intensely blue eyes. 'She deals with temporary staff and—'

'Saskia's been held up, it seems. So, as I'm passing…' He held out his hand. 'Thank you for helping us out. We do appreciate it.'

Jemima transferred her handbag to her other shoulder and held out her own hand. 'You're w-welcome.'

His hand closed over hers in that double handshake thing. The one that was supposed to convey sincerity, but was usually a sign of exactly the opposite. Tall, dark, handsome…actually, very handsome…and completely aware of it.

Everything about him was clean-cut and expensive. His suit was in a dark grey with a faint blue stripe in the weave and it fitted his muscular body as though it had been made for him. Perhaps it had. Jemima didn't know how you judged these things.

It was easy to get the measure of the man himself though. Smooth and sharp. Too smooth… and too sharp. It wasn't by chance he'd selected a tie in a cold ice-blue, a colour that matched his incredibly piercing eyes.

'I'm Miles Kingsley. You'll be working with me.'

Jemima felt her stomach drop and disappear. *This was absolutely not what she wanted. He* was not what she wanted. All the way here on the tube she'd been praying that Miles Kingsley would be a comfortable kind of man and easy to work for.

Amanda had told her that she'd never had a complaint from any temp about working for Miles and, in her mind, she'd pictured him as a controlled, sensible, mature man. Someone not unlike her late father, in fact. Perfect for a woman dipping one very nervous toe back into the job market.

But there was nothing 'comfortable' about this man. He was a cocksure thirty-something who clearly felt he was God's particular gift to the world.

Perhaps Amanda hadn't understood quite what she was looking for in her first job? Or perhaps Amanda had simply decided to drop her firmly in the deep end and see if she swam. That was the trouble with going to an agency owned and run by the sister of your best friend. People who thought they knew you well were all too apt to make decisions they considered to be in your best interests…without reference to what you actually did want.

'I'll take you up to where you'll be working and by then I'm sure Saskia will be free to take you through our procedures.'

'Thank you.'

'Nothing too out of the ordinary, I imagine.'

And then he smiled. A perfect balance of casual warmth and glinting sex appeal. Jemima clutched at her shoulder bag. This was going to be hideous. Miles Kingsley might possibly have hidden neurosis somewhere, but if he did it was deeply buried.

How could any one individual be so completely without…? She searched for the word. So without self-doubt? That was it. He was so darn sure of himself. And all that confidence seemed to suck away what was left of hers. Perhaps she ought to ring Amanda now? Tell her she couldn't do this job?

Jemima frowned. But how pathetic was that?

She'd have to go home and tell her mother she hadn't been able to do it. How did you do that? How did you tell a woman who'd been a senior civil servant until she'd taken early retirement that you couldn't manage a simple temp job? Then she'd have to tell the boys…

And she wanted them to be proud of her. Wanted them to see her taking control of her life again. It would be good for them. Everybody said so.

Miles turned and crossed to the reception desk. 'Felicity, would you hold my calls for the next five minutes or so. And would you let Saskia know I've collected Jemima on my way through.'

'Yes, of course.'

Jemima watched as the receptionist became a pool of hormones at his feet. Assuming she did have hair extensions, one more flick of her lustrous locks and they might fall out. Though, to give him his due, Miles Kingsley didn't appear to notice. Perhaps because ninety-nine point nine per cent of women he met did the same.

'This way,' he said, turning back to her and pointing up the wide glass and steel staircase.

Jemima gave the receptionist a tentative smile and turned to follow him.

'Have you been temping long?'

'No. Not really.' *Or, in fact, not at all.* Probably better not to mention that, though. Jemima clutched at her shoulder bag and swallowed nervously.

'To the left here,' he remarked, pointing down a corridor, 'you'll find a staff recreational room—which is a grand way of saying it's a pleasant place to have a coffee break. Saskia will show you around later and introduce you to the other support staff. We're a tightly knit team and I'm sure they'll all be available to help you, should you need it.'

Jemima nodded.

'This way.' He stepped back and held the door open. 'Do you know much about what Kingsley and Bressington do?'

'Not a great deal,' she replied stiffly. Amanda had concentrated on it being a 'fantastic place to work', and 'I've got temps queuing up to go there. Give it a try and see what you think'. Clearly the smooth and efficient Miles expected she'd have been given a little more information than that.

She let her eyes wander about the total unexpectedness of the place. From the outside it looked like any other Victorian building in the street, but inside…Inside it had been gutted and everything chosen to ensure maximum impact. Small, but perfectly formed, it was all cutting edge and very modern. Intimidating, actually. But that was probably intentional. Anyone hiring Kingsley and Bressington to manage their public persona probably wanted to see something high-tech, stylish and controlled.

'But you've worked in public relations before?'

Jemima shook her head, feeling as though she

were letting Amanda down. She watched the slight frown mar his forehead and wondered, not for the first time, whether Miles Kingsley was the kind of man who'd be satisfied with her newly acquired secretarial skills. As if she didn't know he wasn't.

'There are various aspects to what we do. Some of our clients are large corporations and we track and manage their image in the press, both here and abroad.'

She struggled to suppress the rising tide of panic. A six month post-graduate secretarial course hadn't even begun to touch on anything he was talking about. Somehow she didn't think he'd be particularly impressed that she held a Qualified Private and Executive Secretarial diploma—albeit with a distinction.

'Others are individuals, predominantly working in the media. Many find themselves in a particularly sensitive place in their lives when they first come to us.'

'I see.' Another door, another corridor. It wasn't that the building Kingsley and Bressington occupied was particularly large, it was just it was painted in similar shades of cream and it was difficult to get your bearings. There was only so much limestone and travertine a girl could take.

'Confidentiality is an absolute prerequisite,' Miles continued, 'as I'm sure you realise.'

Confidentiality was something they'd covered in

her diploma course. It was nice to know there was at least one part of this job she was going to find easy. 'I wouldn't dream of repeating anything I learn from working here. I'd consider that very unprofessional.'

'Excellent,' he said, holding open the door for her. 'I know Amanda wouldn't have sent you to us if that wasn't the case. This is your office.'

Jemima stepped through into a room that had obviously been designed to have a *wow* factor. Yet more shades of cream blurred together as a restful whole and made the burr walnut desk a focal point. The computer screen on it was wafer-thin and the chair she recognised as being a modern design classic. A Charles and Ray Eames styled, if not original, chair upholstered in soft cream leather.

'We rarely keep our clients waiting, but if there's any delay I'll rely on you to keep them happy until I can see them.' He turned and pointed to some chairs clustered around yet another shattered glass coffee table. 'Ply them with tea and coffee. Make sure they feel important.'

Jemima felt the first stirrings of a smile. Maybe Amanda had known what she was doing when she had sent her here. She knew a lot about making other people feel important. Being a satellite to other people's bright star was what she did best. In fact, a lifetime of practice had honed it into an art form.

She glanced back towards the door and noticed the twenty or so black and white photographs grouped together on the wall. Dramatic publicity shots all autographed with love and messages of thanks.

Miles followed her gaze. 'Some of our clients,' he said unnecessarily. 'You can see why discretion is imperative.'

She certainly could. Her smile widened as she recognised the chiselled features of an actor who'd scarcely been off the tabloid front pages in recent weeks. His particular 'sensitive place' was a pole-dancer from Northampton—allegedly.

And Kingsley and Bressington had to find a way of spinning that into a positive, did they? She couldn't quite see how that would be possible. If Miles Kingsley could restore that actor's persona as a 'family man', he was a genius.

The door opened and a young and stunning blonde in impeccably cut black trousers burst in, an A4 file tucked under her arm. 'Miles, I'm so sorry. I was caught on the phone and couldn't get away—'

'Jemima had been in reception for over fifteen minutes.' His voice sliced smoothly over the other woman's words.

'Felicity has just buzzed me. I'm so sorry.'

'It's not a problem,' Jemima interjected quickly, unsure whether the apology was for her benefit or for Miles's.

'If you'd like to come with me now, I'll take you through everything.' The other woman adjusted the file under her arm. 'I'm Saskia Longthorne, by the way. Come through to my office….'

She was halfway to the door before she'd finished speaking.

'Jemima might like to hang up her jacket? Put her bag down?' Miles suggested in a dry tone.

He'd strolled over to the walnut desk and had picked up a large black diary and was leafing through the pages. Jemima glanced over as he looked up. His eyes were astonishingly bright against the minimal colour in the room. At least that was her excuse for the sudden tightening of her throat.

'I'll see you again in a few minutes.' He picked up the diary and carried it across to the wide double doors that, presumably, led to his own office.

Good grief. Jemima let out her breath in one slow steady stream. Miles Kingsley was a sharp-suited nightmare. No other way of looking at it.

Saskia seemed to understand what she'd been thinking. 'I know,' she said, walking over to a tall cupboard. 'Miles is a walking force field. You can leave your jacket and handbag in here.' She pulled out a hanger and handed it across. 'It'll be perfectly safe, but there's a key to lock it if you prefer. Zoë always did that…and then kept the key somewhere in her desk.'

'Zoë's the person I'm covering?' Jemima asked, self-consciously slipping her jacket off and putting it on the hanger.

'Her husband's job was transferred to Hong Kong. Just for six weeks, but Miles was as irritated as hell. He thought he'd finally found a PA who didn't seem to want to get pregnant, when Zoë announced she had to be off anyway.'

Saskia accepted back the hanger and popped the jacket into the cupboard. 'Not exactly a "baby-man" is Miles. More wine bar and whisky on the rocks, if you know what I mean.'

That figured, Jemima thought.

'Zoë's lovely so he's holding her job open for her. We mustn't take long over this,' Saskia said, pushing open the door to the corridor. 'He'll want you back quickly. Obviously do put down nine thirty as your start time for today on your time sheet as it's my fault we're a little behind.'

'Jemima, I'm going to need you to book a table at The Walnut Tree for this lunchtime,' Miles said, opening the door to his office, presumably by magic since he had a file under one arm and a mug of black coffee in his other hand.

Jemima tucked her handbag away in the tall cupboard and glanced down at her wrist-watch. Officially she wasn't even supposed to be here yet, but this morning the tube had been kind and the boys cooperative. He was lucky she was here. Jemima hurried across to her desk and jotted down 'Walnut Tree'.

'I've arranged to meet Xanthe Wyn and her agent there at one,' he said, putting the file down on her desk. 'If that's not possible you'll need to contact Christopher Delland to let him know the change.'

'Okay.'

Miles took a sip of his coffee and then raked a hand through his dark hair. 'Actually, confirm it with him anyway. Xanthe is notoriously difficult to pin down. His number is in…' He trailed off as her fingers had already pulled the appropriate card out of the strangely old-fashioned card system her predecessor had favoured.

'Excellent.' Miles flashed her that mega-watt smile that no doubt managed to melt the hardest of hearts, but didn't do anything for her but irritate. Given the choice she would so much rather he left the charm offensive until after ten o'clock when she'd had a chance to wake up properly. Not to mention grab a coffee for herself.

Jemima flicked the switch that would boot up her computer. There was something in the gene pool of men like Miles Kingsley, she thought, which meant they had a deep inner belief that they were somehow special. That when they said 'go' everyone around them would naturally follow. A leader of leaders. It was in the way he moved, walked and owned the space in which he stood.

If he thought one smile would mean she didn't notice the extra ten minutes at the start of the day, the additional twenty minutes at lunch time and the fifteen or so at the end, he was going to be disappointed when she presented her time sheet on Friday.

'Thanks, by the way, for staying late last night.'

'You're welcome,' she said stiffly, finding it annoying to be thanked for something she was busy resenting.

'Amanda didn't say anything about you being fluent in French, but it was extremely useful. Phillipe Armond said your accent is perfect and he was very impressed.'

Jemima smiled through gritted teeth.

'It looks like we're going to get their business. So thanks for that. I'm going to fly to Paris to meet him for lunch some time next week. His secretary will ring you with the arrangements.'

She nodded and picked up the enormous pile of paper that had appeared in her in-tray overnight. If only he'd disappear back into his office. She desperately wanted to grab a coffee before getting started on this lot. She really couldn't be late again tonight.

'Did you have a good evening?'

Jemima looked up incredulously. She'd not left

Kingsley and Bressington until twenty past six. Then she'd had to stand up on the tube all the way home, apologise to her mum, who was going to be late for her bridge evening, listen to Sam read, search out Ben's missing football sock, put another load of washing through the machine…

What did he think her evening was like? Miles Kingsley really had no idea how the other half lived. 'Fine, thanks,' she said, keying in the password.

'I went to see the new production of Noel Coward's *Private Lives*. It's not my favourite play, but it was excellent. That reminds me,' he said, finishing off the last of his coffee. 'Send some flowers to Emma Lawler at Ashworths for me. The address is in that box. I've got an account with Weldon Florists. Ask for Becky.'

Jemima flicked through the 'A' section and pulled out the 'Ashworths' card. She couldn't quite believe he was asking her to do this. One would think he'd manage to send his own girlfriend some flowers and not have to get his secretary to do it for him.

'Not roses. Try for something more…'

'More what?' Jemima asked, her pencil hovering over the pad.

Miles flashed a smile. 'Neutral. Tell Becky it's the end of a beautiful friendship. She'll know what you mean.'

Good grief. Was he really ending a relationship so casually? 'And what message do you want?'

Miles picked up his file. 'The usual. Thanks for a nice evening and I'll be in touch,' he said cheerfully, putting his mug down on her desk. 'When you've got a second, I'd love another coffee. No rush.'

Miles rubbed a tired hand over the back of his neck and listened to the high-pitched panic on the other end of the phone. Some days....

If the blasted woman, and that was putting it mildly, had done as he'd advised there wouldn't *be* a picture of her in the *News of the World*. He let his long fingers idly play with the paper-clips he kept in a small Perspex box. She'd been in the business long enough to know the kind of caption she'd get if she got caught without make-up—so what had possessed her to go out like that? It was hardly rocket science to know there'd be one or two paparazzi, at least, who'd be hanging about on the off chance of their getting something.

Well, it seemed they'd hit the jackpot. No editor alive would have been able to resist pictures like that. He sat back in his chair and mouthed 'coffee' at Jemima, who was coming in with the morning mail.

Did his temporary secretary ever crack a smile? The woman seemed to be perpetually frowning. Or perhaps it was just him that had that effect on her? Jemima was efficient enough, but she wasn't like Zoë and the sooner she was back from Hong Kong the better. Given a choice he really would prefer a bit of humour in his working day.

'Lori,' he interrupted the distressed woman on the other end of the phone, 'there's nothing we can do about pictures that are already in the public domain. I know we've got an injunction out on the topless photographs you did when you were twenty, but this really isn't the same situation and I—'

Miles frowned in irritation as she launched off again. Her famously husky tones transmuted into something quite uncharacteristic. Lori obviously needed to vent her spleen somewhere and he was a safe pair of hands.

'It's not the same situation at all. Lori, you need to keep a low profile at the moment. You and I both know how this works. Give it a couple of weeks and they'll be after the scent of someone else's blood—'

He watched as Jemima came back in to the room carrying his coffee. She'd eased off slightly on the formal clothes since her first morning, but she was still the most 'old before her time' woman he'd met in a long time. She dressed like a woman between forty and fifty and yet he was sure she was younger than that. She could be anywhere between twenty-five and thirty-five.

Miles studied her intently. She probably would look dramatically more attractive if she did something with her hair other than tie it back in a low pony-tail. It was the most amazing colour. A natural redhead. His mouth curved into a sexy smile. It wasn't often you met a *natural* redhead.

'Lori, it'll be two weeks at worst.' He picked up his pen and started to doodle on the A4 pad in front of him—large abstract boxes which he shaded in with swift strokes. Then he wrote 'Keira', around which he put flourishing curlicues. 'If any member of the royal family do anything remotely newsworthy it'll be less than that.'

Jemima placed his coffee in front of him and he looked up to mouth his thanks. It irked him that he couldn't get any real response out of her. She didn't talk about anything personal. Not her husband, nor her children. Nothing. She didn't even seem to have any kind of social life. A question as to what she'd done the night before had elicited a blank look.

And she didn't seem to like him much. Every so often he would catch her watching him with those big green eyes and her expression wasn't complimentary. She seemed to be on the verge between contempt and amusement. All in all, he wasn't sure what to make of her.

He turned his attention back to Lori. 'Just make sure you don't give any kind of statement to the press. Do you understand me? It's very important.'

Miles finished his call and flicked through his mail. There was nothing there that particularly caught his attention and his eyes moved over the doodles he'd drawn on his pad of paper—*Keira*. Keira Rye-Stanford. Now she was one very…sexy woman. That wraparound dress she'd worn last night had seemingly been held together with one very small bow. Just one pull would have…

He stood up and walked over to the door between his office and the outer one. 'Jemima.'

She looked up from the computer screen, a small frown of concentration on her forehead. 'Yes?'

'Would you arrange to have some flowers sent to a Keira Rye-Stanford at—' he pulled the name of her art gallery out from the recesses of his memory '—at Tillyard's. You'll find the address in the directory.'

'Keira Rye-Stanford?'

He could hear the censure in her voice, as though she were reminding him he'd sent flowers to someone entirely different three days earlier. 'That's right.'

'What would you like to send?'

Miles conjured up an image of Keira—a Celtic beauty with a soft Irish lilt and a very seductive glint in her blue eyes. She was a woman who probably received flowers often. And that meant one needed to be creative.

He smiled. 'A dandelion.'

Jemima looked up, her pencil poised on her pad. 'You want to send a dandelion?'

'With a message:

Roses are red, Violets are blue,
This is a Dandelion, but it's for you.

Ask them to wrap it in cellophane with a big bow and deliver it to the reception desk at Tillyard's.'

'A dandelion?'

'Trust me,' he said with a wink as he headed back towards his office, 'it works. Every time.'

Jemima finished writing his message and thumped her pencil down on top of the pad.

He stopped. 'Do you have a problem with that?'

Jemima's green eyes flashed, but she answered smoothly. 'If the florist does, I'll let you know.'

'She won't. She'll just charge me the earth,' he said, shutting the door to his office.

What was Jemima's problem? Anyone would think he was asking her to pick the blasted dandelion herself, instead of picking up the telephone and calling a florist he had an account with. Becks would think it a giggle. He could guarantee she'd make a first rate job of it. Keira would receive a disproportionately large cellophane-wrapped weed tied together with a classy ribbon. Perfect.

His telephone buzzed and he picked up the receiver with a casual, 'Miles.'

'It's an Emma Lawler. She's says it's personal.'
His temporary secretary's voice was bland.

'Thanks, Jemima. Put her through.' Miles sat
back in his chair and waited for Emma's breathless
voice to speak before he said, 'Did you get my flowers?'

CHAPTER TWO

'PLEASE come tonight. It'll be fun. Alistair's best man is going to be here—and he's single.'

Jemima closed her eyes against Rachel's voice. Why did she do this? *Why did everybody do this?*

'You'll like him.'

'I'm not interested in getting involved with anyone else,' Jemima protested weakly, carrying the phone through to the lounge and curling up in one oversized sofa. *Been there, done that and burnt the T-shirt.* The man who could get under her defences was going to have to have more ability than Houdini himself.

'Just because Russell is a complete arse it doesn't mean all men are.'

She knew that, of course she did. Not that Russell was an 'arse', as Rachel put it. If he had been it would have made everything so much easier. He was a nice man—who didn't love her any more. He was very sorry about it, but…

He just didn't. Simple as that, apparently. He'd sat down opposite her in the kitchen one Sunday afternoon and explained that he needed time apart. Time to think about what he wanted from life. Of course, in the end he'd decided he'd rather have a blonde account executive from Chiswick called Stefanie.

How had that happened? Had he woken up one morning and suddenly realised he felt nothing for her? Or had it been something that had come on gradually, almost without him noticing it? Jemima shook her head as though to rid herself of those thoughts. Dissecting every part of their marriage like that was the surest way of going insane. Sometimes she felt as if she was hanging by a thread anyway.

'I'm not trying to pair you up, really. He's not your type.' Rachel's voice seemed to radiate happiness. 'We just thought it would be a nice way of you two meeting before the wedding. The boys are with Russell this weekend, aren't they?'

'Yes.'

'Well, then,' Rachel said, as though that settled everything. 'No point sitting in on your own. Alistair is cooking—so you don't have to worry about food poisoning.'

Jemima gave in to the inevitable. 'Do you want me to bring anything?'

'Just you. Come early. I've been dying to show

you the Jimmy Choo sandals I've chosen to go with my dress. I've had to take out a second mortgage, but they are to die for and since I'm only going to do this once…' She broke off. '*Hell,* I'm sorry. That was really insensitive of me.'

The contrition in her friend's voice brought a smile to her face. 'Don't be daft.' Her finger followed the shape of the agapanthus leaf design on the sofa fabric. 'Alistair's lovely and I'm sure you're going to be very happy together.'

'I really should try and engage my brain before I speak. It's just this wedding stuff is all-encompassing. I don't seem to be able to think about anything else at the moment. It's all dresses, bouquets, flowers, table settings…I'm really sorry. And I haven't even asked you anything about your new job yet. What a cow I am!'

'There's not a lot to tell.' Jemima idly twisted the navy-blue tassel at the corner of the cushion. 'I've only done a couple of weeks.'

And I hate it. I hate being away from the boys. Hate missing meeting up with my friends. Hate my life being *different* from the way I planned it. No point saying any of that. There was no way Rachel would understand how she felt about working at Kingsley and Bressington.

'Are the girls you're working with nice?'

'Girls' was just about the only way to describe them. Jemima thought of Saskia with her board-flat stomach, Lucinda with her exquisite and very large solitaire engagement ring, Felicity with her nails…

'Everyone's very friendly.'

'But?' Rachel prompted. 'Go on, tell me. I can hear it in your voice. How's it going really?'

There was going to be no escape. 'Everyone's incredibly friendly,' she said slowly. 'Just a little young, maybe. I feel a bit like Methuselah.'

'You're only thirty,' Rachel objected. 'And so am I, for that matter! Nothing old about being thirty.'

Jemima smiled. 'Well, I reckon the average age of the female staff is about twelve. Thirteen at the outside. And I don't think there's a woman in the building apart from me who doesn't have prominent hip-bones and the kind of skin that doesn't need foundation. It's all a bit depressing.'

Rachel gave a cackle of laughter. 'You should be used to that. Growing up with Verity as your sister must have been really depressing.'

'You'd think so,' Jemima agreed, 'but honestly, Saskia makes even my sister look fat. They all sit around at lunchtime telling each other they're completely full on a plate of lettuce and make me feel guilty for eating a cheese sandwich. At least Verity moans about being hungry.'

'You're wicked. What about the guy you're working for?'

'England's answer to Casanova?' Jemima said with a sudden smile. 'He's nice enough. Very calm in a crisis, obviously brilliant at his job and completely full of himself. Yesterday he got me to send a dandelion to this poor woman he'd met at a party the night before. Says it works every time…'

Jemima trailed off as she watched her ex-husband's silver BMW drive up the road.

'Did it work?'

'Rachel, I'm going to have to go. I've just seen Russell arriving. I'll see you tonight.'

Jemima finished the call and called out, 'Ben. Sam. Daddy's here.'

She glanced across at the mantelpiece clock. He was five minutes early. He'd now sit in the car until it was *exactly* ten. She hated the way he did that. Why couldn't he be like other absent fathers and gradually drift out of their lives? It would be so much easier if he simply disappeared.

Guilt slid in—as it always did. *She shouldn't have thought that*. She didn't mean it. It was *great* that Russell didn't let his boys down. Turned up when he said he would. *Great* that he paid everything he should—and on time. Really, really *great*.

Jemima uncurled from the sofa and threw the cushion across to the armchair. It just didn't *feel* so great.

'Ben. Sam.' She walked to the foot of the stairs and shouted again. 'Ben? Did you hear me? Daddy's here.'

Ben appeared, shuttered from all emotion.

Almost. His eyes were over-bright and his body was stiff. 'I don't want to go.'

She hated this. 'I know, darling,' she said softly.

'I want to go to the football tournament.' Ben walked slowly down the stairs. 'Everyone's going to be there. Joshua's mum is going to take a picnic.'

'I know, but Daddy has been looking forward to seeing you. He loves his weekends with you.'

The front doorbell rang. Jemima glanced at her wrist-watch. *Exactly* ten o'clock. Not a minute before, not a minute after. Russell was so…*damn* reasonable.

She looked at Ben as he picked up his bag. 'It'll be fun when you're there.' What a stupid thing to say. That wasn't the point. Ben was eight years old and he wanted to play football with his friends. *Of course* he did…

'You'll be okay.'

He nodded.

'And you'll have a really great time.'

Ben put his backpack on his shoulders. 'What are you going to do, Mum?'

'Me?' *What was she going to do without them?* Cry a little… Miss them a lot… The same as every other weekend they spent with their father. 'I'm going to spend the day trying to decorate the bathroom, maybe get some tiles up, and then I'm going to go and have supper with Rachel and Alistair. I'll be fine.' She forced a bright smile and wondered how convincing she was. 'It's not long. Just one night and you'll be home again.'

The doorbell rang again.

'Will you go and hurry Sam up for me?'

She watched him climb the stairs and counted to ten before she opened the front door. It didn't matter how prepared she thought she was, seeing Russell always felt strange. In the space of a millisecond she remembered the first time he'd kissed her, the proposal in a felucca in Vienna, the way he'd cried when Ben was born…

Russell looked good. Clearly he'd decided to keep up his gym membership and she liked the way he'd let his hair grow a little longer. Jemima wrapped her arms protectively around her waist. 'Ben's just gone to find Sam. They're all ready.'

Russell nodded. 'There's no hurry.' Silence and then, 'How are things?'

'Fine.'

Another pause. 'That's excellent.' He rattled his car keys and looked uncomfortable.

He always did that too, Jemima thought. *What exactly did he think she was going to do?* Cry? Scream at him? He flattered himself. She was a long way past that. 'You?'

'Yes, well, we're fine.' He stood a little straighter. 'Stef's just got a promotion…'

'That's…great.'

'She's heading up a team of three.'

Jemima nodded. She was proud of herself for being so grown-up and dignified. But why exactly did Russell think she'd be interested in the career progression of the woman he'd left them for? *No*, she corrected swiftly. The woman he'd left *her* for.

'Daddy!' Sam hurled himself along the hallway. 'It's Daddy!'

The change in Russell was instantaneous. The smile on his face gripped her heart and screwed it tight. He reached down and caught the tornado. 'Hiya, imp.'

'I've lost another tooth.' Sam pulled a wide grin, showing a huge expanse of pure gum.

'Did the tooth fairy come?'

Ben pushed past. 'There's no such thing. It's Mum. No one believes in the tooth fairy any more.'

Above his head Russell met her eyes. Jemima gave a half smile, then a shrug. 'Have a good time.' She reached out and touched Ben's head. 'I'll see you tomorrow.'

Then she had to watch the three of them walk to the car.

She really hated this.

Still.

How many weekends had it been now? Was there ever going to be a time when it didn't feel as if part of her was being ripped out of her body when she saw her sons walk away? She felt exactly like a piece of string which had been pulled so tight it had started to fray.

Miles locked his Bristol 407 and sauntered over to the three-storey Victorian house where Alistair and Rachel had bought their first flat together. It was nice. High ceilings, plenty of original features, good area…and that oh, so rare commodity—outside space in the form of a tiny courtyard garden.

Normally he really enjoyed his visits to their home. Every so often it was pleasant to spend an evening where there were no demands placed on him, no expectations. They were a calm oasis in a life that was becoming increasingly pressured.

But…

He pulled a face. Truth be told, he wasn't entirely looking forward to the next few hours. An evening spent discussing weddings wasn't exactly high on his list of favourite things to do with a Saturday night. But hey…

He reached up and rang the bell. If his old school friend had finally decided to take the plunge, the least he could do was be there to see it. The poor beggar probably only had a year or so before their country place in Kent was filled with bright plastic toys and the first of several mini-Mackenzies. Grim.

The door opened suddenly and Rachel met him with a bright smile. 'I thought you'd be Jemima,' she said, glancing up the tree-lined street. 'I wonder where she's got to. I bet her car is playing up. She was coming early to look at my shoes.'

'Would you like me to look at your shoes?' he asked lazily.

Rachel turned back to him. 'You behave or I'll make you wear a pink floral waistcoat! Go on in.'

'For you—anything,' he glinted, leaning forward to place a light kiss on her cheek.

'You'll find Alistair in the kitchen doing something clever with the duck.'

She shut the door behind him and Miles shrugged out of his tan leather jacket and threw it over the oak church chair they kept in the hall. 'So, tell me, will I fancy the bridesmaid?'

'Quite possibly—' she grinned up at him '—but I doubt it'll be reciprocated. She's a woman of taste and discernment. Actually, I don't think I have any friends who would deign to join your harem.'

Miles smiled and wandered through to where Alistair was stirring something in a small saucepan. He looked up as his friend walked in. 'Talking about Jemima?'

'He wants to know whether he'll fancy her,' Rachel said, leaning over to see how the sauce looked. 'Should it be that lumpy?' Then, as the doorbell rang, 'That'll be her. Excellent.'

Alistair watched her leave with an expression of

amusement and turned back to his sauce. '*Lumpy!*
Just about escaped with her life. Miles, grab
yourself a drink.'

Miles sauntered over and poured himself out
a large glass of red wine from the bottle on the
side. 'You?'

'Got one,' Alistair said, with a nod at the glass
by his side. 'How's work? I saw Lori Downey's
double page spread and thought you might be
having it tough.'

Miles grunted and took a mouthful of the full-
bodied wine. 'This is nice.'

'Rachel and I got it in Calais last month. Our car
was so laden it's a wonder we weren't stopped.' In
the hallway they could hear the mumble of female
voices. 'Sounds like Jemima's here at last.'

Miles perched on a high bar stool, feeling more
relaxed than he had done all week. He set his wineglass down on the side and idly started stirring the
sugar in the bowl. 'I've got a Jemima temping for
me at the moment. Amanda sent her to me.'

'Good?'

'She's fine.'

Alistair smiled. 'Damned with faint praise.'

'Something like that. You can't fault what she
does when she's in the office, but she arrives at the
last possible moment and leaves as soon as she can.
Doesn't talk. Doesn't socialise with the girls.' Miles
picked up his wineglass. 'She dresses like her

mother and obviously thinks my florist bill is too high.'

'Can't blame her for that. Rachel thinks your florist bill is too high.'

The voices from the hall became louder.

Miles watched as Alistair carefully decanted his sauce into a jug. 'That doesn't say much for Rachel's judgement. Are you sure about marrying her?'

Alistair laughed. 'One of the most attractive things about Rachel is that she prefers me to you. Go easy on the futility of marriage stories tonight. Jemima's been through a traumatic divorce. Russell left her with a house to renovate and two boys to bring up on her own. She's a bit brittle.'

'So I'm not even allowed to flirt with the brides-maid—' He broke off as soon as the door opened, but he could see from Alistair's face that he thought they may have been overheard. He felt a vague sense of sympathy. If he knew anything about women—and he did—Rachel would have her fiancé's kneecaps for that *fauxpas*.

'Miles—' Rachel's voice sounded ominously clipped '—this is Jemima. My bridesmaid.'

He turned round, ready to pour oil on troubled waters…and felt his smile falter. It was as if he'd stepped through a portal to an alternative universe. *Rachel was standing with her arm tucked through Jemima Chadwick's.*

And, stranger than that, Jemima Chadwick as he'd never seen her before.

Her red hair was a riot of curls and she was dressed in a simple linen sundress. She looked crumpled, curvy and surprisingly sexy. He felt that familiar kick in the pit of his abdomen that was pure reflex. It was all a bit surreal.

'This is Miles Kingsley. Alistair and Miles were at school together and, scarily, have known each other for something like thirty years.'

Somehow he couldn't get his mouth to work. Thoughts were whizzing through his head, but they didn't stay still long enough to know whether they were worth putting words on. Even a simple hello seemed to elude him.

Alistair leapt into action, clearly motivated to bonhomie by the 'brittle' mistake. 'Absolutely right. Miss Henderson's class. Aged five. Abbey Preparatory School, Windsor. What can I get you to drink, Jemima?'

She moved further into the room. 'White wine would be lovely. Thank you.'

Jemima Chadwick.

Here.

And looking so different. Smelling of…roses. Her red curls still damp…

Miles found that his mind was thinking in expletives. It was almost unbelievable that Jemima Chadwick could have transformed herself so entirely. The woman who'd left the office on Friday evening bore very little resemblance to the one who'd arrived for dinner tonight.

At work she looked...bland. Completely invisible, as though she didn't expect to be looked at. In fact, very *married*. His eyes flicked to her ring finger. Nothing. He'd not noticed that. He hadn't noticed she had legs like that either...

Miles took a sip of wine and tried to recall exactly what he'd said about his temporary secretary to Alistair...and then he winced. Thank God he could trust Alistair not to land him in it when he realised they'd been speaking about the same Jemima.

Damn. This couldn't be happening to him.

What was the probability of Jemima Chadwick being Rachel's bridesmaid? It had to be zillions to one. Except, of course, she was Rachel's friend and Amanda was Rachel's elder sister. *Damn it!* It wasn't so much improbable as extremely likely.

Alistair poured out a glass of wine. 'Miles was just saying he's got a temporary secretary working for him at the moment who's also called Jemima.'

Miles felt his stomach drop. It was the same feeling as when your dinghy was about to capsize and there was absolutely nothing you could do to stop it. He was going over. It was inevitable.

'That's quite a coincidence. It's not a particularly common name, is it?' Alistair continued, sublimely oblivious to the missile he was hurling in their midst.

'I heard.' Jemima looked directly at Miles. Her green eyes were steady, like lasers. 'She dresses like her mother.'

Miles's head jerked up.

It was like receiving a swift left to his chin. So quick he hadn't seen it coming. It hadn't occurred to him that Jemima could have heard what he'd said about her. In his adult life there'd probably only been a handful of occasions when he'd wanted the ground to open up and swallow him whole. This was one of those occasions. It was up there in number one slot along with the time his mother had given a television interview explaining that he'd been conceived in a moment of 'peace and meditation'.

Rachel reached out for her own wine. 'Jemima's just started temping. Perhaps she ought to work for you, Miles.'

This was getting worse. Miles's eyes searched out Jemima's, a desperate apology in his own.

He watched the indecision as it passed across her green eyes. Then she gave a half smile and held out her hand. 'It's lovely to meet you.'

His sense of relief was overwhelming. 'And you,' he said, stretching out his own hand. 'Jemima…?'

'Chadwick.'

It was fascinating to see the sudden spark of laughter light her eyes. What was it they said about still waters running deep?

'Jemima Chadwick.'

His hand closed round hers. On the whole he thought she'd made the right choice. It was far easier to pretend they didn't know each other. He was more than happy to go along with that. And, at the first opportunity, he'd apologise.

'The man she's working for sounds worse than you, Miles,' Rachel said. 'Apparently he sent some woman a dandelion. Or rather he got Jemima to do it.'

Miles watched a red stain appear on Jemima's neck and gradually spread to her cheeks. It seemed that fate had struck a blow for equality. 'Sounds fun,' he said, releasing her hand.

The flush became a little darker. 'I'm told it works every time,' she shot back quickly.

'He sounds a jerk,' was Alistair's observation. 'Shall we go out to the garden? We've set everything out there as it's a nice evening.'

Miles led the way outside, not sure how he was feeling any more. Honesty compelled him to admit that Jemima carried the advantage in the cringe stakes. The things he'd said about her to Alistair were completely out of order—regardless of whether she'd overheard them. His mother would have him flayed alive for comments like that. As long as Jemima did her job properly there was no reason why she should socialise or dress differently. No reason at all.

Nevertheless it was a mystery to him why someone who could look as…downright sexy as Jemima, would go to work looking like everyone's image of the worst kind of librarian. Why do it?

Her work clothes were too safely conventional, but the difference was mainly due to her hair. How had a nondescript pony-tail become a riot of curls? She looked as if she'd stepped out of a pre-Raphaelite painting. All curves, cleavage and abandonment. Perhaps better not to allow his mind to go too far down that particular avenue. Single mums were absolutely out of bounds. Too much baggage. Far too many responsibilities.

He took the seat opposite her, the little devil on his shoulder prompting him to ask, 'So, you're temping?'

Jemima shot him a warning glance, but he didn't care. With Rachel listening in, she'd have to answer him. Who knew what he might find out about her? If you were going to have an excruciatingly embarrassing evening, you might as well turn it to your advantage. Salvage whatever enjoyment you could.

'Yes.'

'As a secretary?' he continued blandly.

It was worth it for the flick of those green eyes. 'Yes.'

'Are you enjoying it?'

Jemima reached out and took a breadstick. She snapped it in half. 'No.'

'Why's that?'

She looked at him and shook her head as though she were warning him off.

'It's because it's her first job,' Rachel chipped in.

First job. Now that was interesting. Miles let his eyebrows raise a fraction and watched with complete enjoyment the blush that heated her face.

Alistair picked up his wine and stood up. 'I'm sure that's right, Jemima. It's a huge lifestyle change for you. Your hair looks great, by the way. I've not seen you leave it curly for months.'

Jemima self-consciously touched her hair. Miles watched as she twisted one strand around her fore-finger. She had no idea what that simple movement of one finger was doing to him. 'I didn't have time to straighten it. I had an argument with a paint pot and the paint pot won.'

'It looks great,' Alistair said as he headed back towards the kitchen.

Rachel nodded. 'I keep telling her.' She looked at Miles. 'She won't listen. She thinks it looks more sophisticated straight.'

He wasn't about to enter that debate, but he was in no doubt which he preferred. 'It's a great colour,' he said softly, willing her to look at him.

She wasn't having any of it. 'It's red,' Jemima

said, picking up her wineglass. 'And the bane of my life.'

Did she really think that? It was unbelievable. He watched as her fingers played with the stem of her wineglass. Nice fingers. Short, tidy nails with no polish on them. That was more in keeping with the Jemima Chadwick he knew.

'So,' he said after a short pause, 'you're in your *first* job…?'

'After my divorce.' She looked at him then and there was no mistaking the warning light in her green eyes. 'It's a shame I'm not enjoying it more, isn't it?'

His lips twitched. 'Why aren't you?'

'My boss is very…smug. Do you know the kind of man I mean? Very difficult to take seriously.'

Her green eyes were…incredible. Why hadn't he noticed them before? Tiny flecks of topaz worked out from dark irises. Two weeks—ten days—sitting in his office and he hadn't noticed. He was slipping.

And she thought him *smug*—apparently. Miles smiled. He probably deserved that. Even so… 'When you've had a little more experience, perhaps you ought to consider working with me. I must speak to Amanda about it.'

Her eyes narrowed and Miles waited to see what she would do next. She took her time and snapped off another piece of breadstick before saying, 'I don't know whether I'd be interested. What is it that you do exactly?'

'Public relations.'

She wrinkled her nose. 'That's a form of professional lying, isn't it?'

'Jemima!' Rachel exclaimed, shocked.

Miles laughed and raised his glass in a mock toast. *Round one to the lady.* How surprising. He took a sip of his wine and placed the glass back on the table. 'So, Jemima,' he began and watched with enjoyment the way she tensed, 'how do you know Rachel?'

'We were at university together,' Rachel answered for her. 'Jemima and I met during freshers week and ended up sharing a house together in our second and third years. Do you remember the house we had first?' she asked, turning to Jemima. 'I swear it had mould in the corner of every room. It even smelt damp.'

'What did you study?' Miles asked.

Those green eyes flashed up at him, clearly resenting telling him anything. It added a little spice to the evening.

'English and French.'

'We both did,' Rachel chimed in. 'Except, of course, Jemima got a first, whereas I got a 2:1.'

Which rather begged the question—what the blazes was she doing working for little more than the minimum wage in a temporary secretarial job? It was none of his business, but his curiosity was piqued.

And, if he was honest, a little more than that. 'So how come you're temping? I'd have thought a first in English and French from Warwick would have led you in an entirely different direction.'

'She meant to be an editor. But then she met Russell and...' Rachel shrugged '...everything changed.'

'So...you gave up everything for love?'

There was a toss of that incredible hair and then she met his eyes. 'I gave up everything when I had my first son,' she corrected him firmly. 'Not that there was much to give up. I was only twenty-one and hadn't had a chance to get started on anything.'

'And now you're picking up where you left off.'

'Hardly,' she shot back with a flash of those incredible eyes, her resentment shimmering across the table towards him. 'When I left off I'd just got a job as an assistant editor with a small educational publisher. Now I'm a temporary secretary. If life's a game of snakes and ladders I've just gone down that really big snake on square twenty-four.'

Alistair was wrong. Jemima Chadwick wasn't *brittle*, she was angry. It seemed that life had hit her particularly hard. Alistair had described her divorce as 'traumatic', but then Miles had never witnessed a divorce that wasn't.

In his circle the accepted opinion was that ex-wives were avaricious and bled their former spouses dry. This was the flip side of that, he supposed. His smile twisted. Jemima had been left with no career to speak of and two children to bring up alone. That was tough. No wonder she was angry.

Rachel topped up Jemima's wine. 'I still think you ought to think about—'

Alistair interrupted by carrying out a large platter of salmon. 'Nigella Lawson swears this is the easy way to entertain. Just fork up what you want. The duck may be a disaster so I wouldn't hold back.'

Rachel stood up and cleared away her central table decoration to make space. She looked around for somewhere to put it.

'Put it behind me,' Jemima suggested. 'It won't get knocked round here.'

Rachel handed over the stunning arrangement of white hydrangea, viburnum and tulips. 'Thanks.'

'You know this is gorgeous. You could do something like it for the wedding,' Jemima suggested, deliberately steering the topic of conversation into a new direction.

In her opinion, Miles Kingsley had spent long enough enjoying himself at her expense. Even talking about weddings was preferable to the continual haemorrhaging of her private business. She pulled back her chair and placed the flowers carefully on the ground. 'All these tea lights are very romantic too.'

Rachel sat down eagerly. 'I was wondering about that. I think it would work really well with our theme—' she sat back to add gravitas to her announcement '—which is going to be…medieval.'

Medieval. That wasn't what Rachel had been talking about for the past four months. 'What happened to "nineteen-forties Hollywood glamour"?'

Miles moved his chair. 'Am I supposed to be understanding any of this?'

'I find it better not to try,' Alistair said, resting an arm along the back of Rachel's chair.

His fiancée smiled at him. 'We've managed to get Manningtree Castle. They've had a cancellation and slotted us in. It's going to be beautiful.'

And an incredible amount of work, Jemima added silently. Manningtree Castle was probably the most romantic place on earth to get married, but it wasn't a package deal by any stretch of the imagination. As far as she could recall from their initial research into the options, Manningtree Castle provided little more than the Norman keep itself and a grassy field with permission to erect a marquee.

'Where's Manningtree Castle?' Miles asked.

Jemima glanced across at him. 'Kent. It's not so much a castle as a bit of one.'

'And it's not far from where Rachel and I bought our cottage. A couple of miles. No more than that,'

Alistair added. 'They're booked up a good eighteen months in advance so we were surprised when they called us to say they'd had a cancellation for the weekend we'd enquired about.'

'Can't you just imagine all those tea lights in the stone alcoves?' Rachel's eyes danced with excitement. 'Or even big church candles. It's going to be stunning.'

'But your invitations—'

Rachel brushed her friend's objection aside. 'We'll just have to resend them.'

Not to mention hire a marquee, find a caterer and local florist to decorate the keep, Jemima thought dryly. She sat back in her chair and made a determined effort not to let what she was feeling show. In her opinion, three months before a wedding was far too late to be changing the venue.

Jemima gave half an ear to her friend as she continued to lay out her artistic vision of a medieval wedding with a distinctly twenty-first century twist. No mention of the halter-neck dress in soft white satin she'd chosen four weeks earlier. What was happening about that?

She wanted to be excited for Rachel, she really did, but it all seemed rather pointless. So much effort for one day…

She speared a piece of salmon from the central platter. She was being selfish. Just because her marriage hadn't been the happy ever after she'd hoped for wasn't a good enough reason not to enter into someone else's excitement. It was just difficult to summon up much enthusiasm for all this nonsense. That probably made her a horrible person, certainly a lousy choice of bridesmaid, but if she didn't say it aloud, just thought it—that wasn't *so* bad, was it?

Jemima glanced across at Miles and caught him watching her. She had the strangest feeling he'd been able to read her mind. That was impossible, of course, but…there was a definite look of… something in his blue eyes.

She turned back to concentrate on her salmon, feeling slightly shaken. Perhaps she'd been imagining it? On the other hand, perhaps they shared a mutual cynicism for big white weddings? She couldn't believe he'd be particularly interested in the finer details of how Rachel intended to decorate the marquee.

Jemima risked a second look. He was listening to Rachel and, whatever his opinion of it all was, he was making a reasonable job of looking fascinated. He really was impossibly handsome. Strange how two eyes, a nose and a mouth could look so different from one person to another. He had a good chin too. Her mum would say it was strong and characterful, but what she particularly liked about it was the small indentation in the centre. It was kind of sexy.

Grief. What had made her think that? Jemima

pulled herself up a little straighter. There was nothing sexy about a man who knew he was sexy. If that made any sense. Miles was too gorgeous. No woman wanted to be with a man who spent more time looking in the mirror than she did.

Actually that was unfair. Miles didn't seem a vain man. He just was drop dead gorgeous. An accident of nature.

She really shouldn't blame him for that. It wasn't his fault any more than it was Verity's that she'd inherited the enviable bone structure and the ability to survive on half a grape.

'Jemima?'

She heard her name and looked up to find Rachel looking at her.

'You're off with the fairies. What are you thinking about?'

Thinking about? 'Um—' Jemima hunted for something to say '—um…' Opposite her, Miles's eyes were alight with laughter. Please God he didn't know *what* she'd been thinking. She cast about for something likely. 'Um…I was wondering what you were going to do about your dress? Surely it's too late to change it now?'

Rachel smiled. 'I was worried about that, but I rang the designer the second I heard Manningtree Castle was available. It's not a problem. And she's caught the vision absolutely.' She gave a delighted laugh. 'I'm so excited. It's going to be perfect.'

'As is my duck. I hope.' Alistair began to gather together their plates.

Rachel picked up the central platter. 'It had better be. He started soaking the apricots last night and he'll be very sulky if it hasn't worked.' She followed Alistair back into the kitchen and Jemima was left alone with Miles.

'Liar,' he said softly.

Jemima looked up. 'Pardon?'

Miles's eyes glinted with wicked amusement. 'You were not wondering about Rachel's dress.'

A smile tugged at the corner of her mouth. 'Did it show?'

'Not to Rachel, it seems. You live to daydream another day.' There were gales of laughter from the kitchen. Miles looked over his shoulder and then turned back to her, saying quietly, 'Do you think she's going to ask me to wear tights and a tunic?'

'If she does,' Jemima whispered back, 'you can console yourself that it's only marginally worse than a russet-coloured waistcoat made from the fabric of my bridesmaid dress.'

The look of complete horror that passed over his face made her laugh and she was still laughing when Alistair and Rachel returned.

'What's so funny?' Rachel asked as she put a warm plate in front of each of them.

'Nothing.'

Miles cast Rachel a baleful look that was

intended to charm. 'Are Alistair and I going to be wearing tights?'

'Absolutely not,' Alistair said, putting his masterpiece in the centre of the table. 'I don't have the calves for it. Now this…is Duck Breasts with Blackberry and Apricot Sauce.'

'Do please notice the elegant presentation,' his fiancée teased, looking up at him. 'Particularly the apricot halves, watercress and blackberry garnish. It was very fiddly.'

The look of love and affection that passed between them suddenly made Jemima feel lonely. Most of the time she managed perfectly well, but just occasionally it spread through her like ink in water.

Rachel sat down. 'You know, Alistair, I think you've got great calves. What about wearing tights?'

CHAPTER THREE

THE Duck Breasts with Blackberry and Apricot Sauce was a triumph, but the Poached Figs with Macaroons and Mascarpone Alistair had lovingly prepared for dessert was less successful. He was entirely philosophical about it and was threatening to invite them all back for a retry later in the month.

Jemima stirred brown sugar crystals into her coffee, surprisingly relaxed. This was so much better than staying home to decorate the bathroom, which had been her original plan for the evening. She'd almost forgotten the trail of 'welkin blue' footprints she'd left spread across the new vinyl floor when she'd tripped over the paint pot lid. She'd even managed to forget that Alistair thought she was 'brittle' and Miles had said that she dressed like her mother.

She sipped the dark liquid and let the flavours travel over her tongue. *Brittle?* Did she really come across as brittle? She didn't want to be seen as brittle. She hadn't known Alistair thought that about her. Rachel had never said.

It was probably true, though. No one knew how painful a divorce was unless they'd first-hand experience of it. It felt as if…you were being physically ripped in half. There was no other way of describing it. Her whole life, everything she'd invested in and worked for, had been shredded as though none of it had mattered. Anyone would be a little 'brittle' after that. *Wouldn't they?*

'Mint?'

She looked up to find Miles was holding out a plate of gold-wrapped mints. Jemima took one.

'Rachel? Do you want one?'

'Thank you.'

Jemima slowly unwrapped the foil-covered mint and let the conversation swirl around her. Miles Kingsley had turned out to be good company. At work he seemed…well…a complete caricature of what she'd imagined a playboy would be like.

It offended her that he seemed to select his dates with no more care than you would make a decision between a chocolate with a cream-filled centre and one with a nutty coating. Even more offensive was the way he discarded them days later, with as little thought.

It seemed the chase was what interested him. Winning. It was as though he were playing some complicated game of his own devising, and when he'd won he lost interest.

Not surprisingly, it wasn't that simple. Miles was a much more complicated man. She'd wanted to dislike him, but she'd not been able to. Jemima spread out the foil wrapper and gently smoothed out the creases.

Maybe it was no more than that she disliked being at Kingsley and Bressington so much that it coloured her opinion of anything and everyone there. Tonight she had to admit that Miles had been fun. Kind, too. If discussing the various merits of a chocolate wedding cake over a traditional fruit one had bored her, it must surely have pushed him close to the edge.

In any case, she thought, smoothing out the final crease, his erudite endorsement of an assortment of cheeses and warm bread in favour of any cake had her vote.

Miles's low laugh made her look up. 'I haven't seen anyone do that since school,' he said, holding out his mint wrapper to her.

Jemima looked back down at the perfectly smooth gold square and back into his laughing blue eyes. A hard lump seemed stuck in her throat.

He had the most amazing eyes. *So sexy.* She felt like a rabbit caught in the glare of oncoming headlights. She couldn't look away. Couldn't speak either.

'I used to do that,' Rachel said, spreading her own wrapper out in front of her. 'It always used to rip, though.'

Alistair leant back in his chair. 'That's because you rush it. Jemima's got patience.'

Finally Jemima managed to find her voice, albeit a huskier one than usual. 'Jemima's got two boys who need amusing when they go out to Sunday lunch. I make a pretty good job of putting After Eight Mint envelopes inside each other too.'

She took Miles's wrapper and carefully eased out the creases. She was aware of Miles's soft laughter and Rachel's cry of irritation when her wrapper tore. Jemima kept her eyes focused on the gold paper until the last crease disappeared and she was left with a shiny square.

'Beautifully done,' Miles said softly.

He made even that sound seductive. No wonder he had women falling over themselves to go out to dinner with him. Like lemmings on a cliff...

Daft. She didn't like to think how dreadful they must feel when he didn't phone, didn't make any effort to contact them again.

Alistair reached out for a mint. 'So, what kind of wedding will you have, Miles? When the time comes.'

'Shotgun,' he answered quickly amid raucous laughter. '*If* the time comes.'

Rachel screwed up her foil wrapper in exasperation and placed it on her plate. 'It'll come. Some woman will sneak up on you and you'll be up the aisle before you know it.'

'She'll have to be SAS trained,' Miles said lazily. 'I think I've got my defences in place.'

He wasn't joking. Miles clearly enjoyed his life exactly as it was, Jemima thought. As long as there were women out there foolish enough to risk their hearts spending time with him, he'd probably go on enjoying it. Why wouldn't he?

Jemima glanced down at her wrist-watch and noticed with surprise how very late it was. The candles dotted around the courtyard had come into their own, but it was beginning to feel cold. She rubbed at her arms.

'Are you getting chilly?' Rachel asked. 'Perhaps we'd better move inside.'

She shook her head. 'It's late. I ought to be going home.'

'Now?'

Jemima held out her wrist to show her watch. 'It's nearly eleven. It's going to take me half an hour to get back.'

'You can't go yet. I've not shown you my shoes,' Rachel protested.

'You can't go before she's done that,' Alistair concurred. 'Miles, more coffee?'

Within minutes she'd been taken to the guest room and Rachel had carefully shut the door. 'Sit on the bed,' she said, opening the wardrobe and reaching up to the top shelf.

Jemima sat down on the deep red eiderdown. Rachel carried the shoe box over and perched next to her. She opened the box as though it contained a live thing. Inside, loving packaged in tissue paper, was a pair of exquisite shoes. They were the colour of rich clotted cream and had seriously pointed toes. Not exactly medieval, but Jemima could see why Rachel had fallen in love with them.

'Are they comfortable?'

Rachel laughed. 'Don't be daft. They're beautiful.'

There was a rap on the door.

'Don't come in,' Rachel shouted, hurrying to put the shoe box back at the top of the wardrobe.

Alistair's voice sounded through the closed door. 'Come on out of there, you two. Miles is about to leave.'

'I'm just coming.' She smiled across at Jemima. 'I can't believe I'm getting married. Can you believe it? I'm so excited.'

Jemima smiled back, but was relieved when Rachel turned away to open the bedroom door. It was hard to keep up the façade that any of this mattered. In reality, married life had nothing to do with the choice of shoes.

As Jemima picked her handbag from off the bed she heard Rachel say, 'Miles, do you really have to go now?'

'I'm afraid I do.'

'Me too.' Jemima appeared in the doorway.

'You're both very boring,' Rachel said, tucking beneath Alistair's arm.

Miles picked up his leather jacket from the hall chair and shrugged himself into it. His black jeans and thick black T-shirt had been sharp, but the jacket took it up another notch. Jemima looked away.

He was actually, she thought, a terrifying kind of man. Too gorgeous to be real, more like someone who'd been airbrushed to perfection.

Instinctively she smoothed down the hopelessly creased linen of her dress and immediately hoped he hadn't noticed. She glanced up at him and caught the wicked glint in his eyes—whatever that meant.

'It was lovely to meet you, Miles,' she said hurriedly, aware her voice sounded slightly breathy.

The glint in his eyes intensified. 'You, too.' He leant forward to kiss her cheek. 'Unexpected, but…lovely.'

It was no more than a peck, but Jemima hadn't anticipated the way it would feel. His hand was strong and warm against her arm and his lips seemed to burn on her cheek. When he stepped back it was as much as she could do not to raise a hand to her face. She glanced over at him, wondering whether he'd noticed anything, hoping he hadn't, but female enough to be irritated when he seemed not to have.

'Thanks for a great evening,' he said as he kissed Rachel before turning and placing a casual slap on Alistair's left shoulder.

Jemima forced herself to move. 'It was fun.' She reached up to kiss Alistair's cheek. 'And the food was delicious.'

Alistair smiled down at her. 'Not the figs.'

'Agreed,' Miles said as he opened the front door. 'The figs need work.'

'I'll ring you,' was Rachel's parting shot. 'I'll arrange another evening when we can all get to-gether.'

'That'll be good,' Miles said, stepping out on to the pavement.

Jemima followed. As the door closed she took a deep breath and stopped to rummage through her handbag for her car keys.

'You survived,' Miles remarked.

She glanced up to find him standing a few feet away from her and her stomach flipped over at the lazy laughter in his blue eyes. Whatever it was he had, he really should bottle it. It was intoxicating. 'So did you.'

'But I was saved the shoe ordeal. Are they par-ticularly medieval, would you say?'

Jemima choked on an unexpected laugh. 'I think a twelfth century peasant might have struggled with the three-inch heels, but…' She smiled. 'Rachel's going to look beautiful…which, I suppose, is the idea.'

He made a noise that sounded remarkably like a 'humph'. 'Alistair will think she looks stunning if she turns up in jeans. He can't believe his luck she's agreed to marry him.' He pulled out his own car keys from his jacket pocket. 'I'm inclined to think they'll be all right, buck the statistics, don't you? They seem good together.'

Jemima glanced back at the blue-painted front door. 'Yes. They are,' she said slowly, turning back to him. 'Really good together.' Then. 'I— I'm sorry I said anything about the dandelion. I shouldn't have—'

'You're apologising to me?' he interrupted, seemingly surprised. Then he smiled. 'It worked, you know. Dinner date on Friday. Keira rang as soon as the delivery hit her desk.'

Jemima's eyes widened. 'Good grief.'

The lines at the sides of Miles's eyes crinkled. 'Wouldn't have been so successful with you, then?'

'Absolutely not!' Jemima smiled up at him. 'I'd probably have sent you back a daisy. Can't think of a rhyme at the moment, but I'm sure I'd have come up with something suitably scathing.'

The blue eyes took on a deeper glint. She loved the way they did that. It made her feel irresponsible, somehow.

'That would have been irresistible.'

He was only teasing—but he was *very* sexy. Jemima looked away. It was going to make Monday morning a bit difficult. She'd preferred it when she'd been able to keep him in a nice, safe mental box marked 'temporary boss—self-assured philanderer'.

'Where are you parked?'

It took a moment before she understood what he'd asked. 'Oh, not far. Just down there.' She nodded down the pavement.

'I'll walk you down.'

'There's no need, I—'

'It's late,' he said, cutting across her, 'it's dark and even my mother would think it okay to accept.'

'Your mother?' Jemima said, confused. What had his mother got to do with anything?

The lines at the edges of his eyes crinkled. 'You don't know?'

She shook her head. *Didn't know what, exactly?*

'My mother's Hermione Kingsley. I would have thought Rachel would have told you. Most people can't resist it.'

Jemima knew she looked blank for a moment and then she clicked who Hermione Kingsley was. Serious journalist and staunch feminist. Perhaps the most famous single parent of them all… Her thought processes clicked up another gear. 'In that case, you must be…' she said slowly.

'Exactly.' He nodded, his eyes once again alight with laughter. 'A social experiment and the most public product of a sperm donation bank.'

Jemima wasn't quite sure what her reaction should be. She hadn't expected he'd say anything like that.

'She tells me it's something to be proud of and I like to think she put a great deal of effort into her choice of donor.'

'I imagine you do,' she replied a little primly and he burst out laughing. 'W-what?'

Miles shook his head, still laughing. 'And you really hope she washed her hands after…'

'I didn't say that,' Jemima protested, her own lips twitching.

'At least you don't have to feel guilty about letting me walk you to your car. Even my mother believes that personal safety has to take precedence over higher ideals of equality.'

'I suppose if your mother approves.'

His answering glint had her stomach twisting itself into knots. It really was no wonder he could get away with sending a dandelion. She had the strongest feeling he could get away with practically anything.

Her car really was only a few paces down the road. Jemima stopped next to her battered Volvo. 'This is it,' she said self-consciously.

Not by so much as a flicker did his eyes give

away his opinion of her car. That took some skill, as it was a complete rust heap. She put her key in the lock and turned it.

'Look,' he said after a short pause, 'I'm really sorry about…earlier. I was out of order.'

Jemima looked over her shoulder. 'That's okay.'

'It isn't. It was crass.'

She straightened up. 'Okay, it was crass,' she agreed with a smile, 'but you didn't know I was standing in the doorway.'

'No, but… Just how much of what Alistair and I were saying did you overhear?'

He looked more uncomfortable than she'd ever seen him. *Not so pleased with himself this time.* It was funny. 'Pretty much all of it.' Miles groaned and Jemima laughed. 'I got the bit about my clothes looking like my mother's—'

'You look lovely tonight,' he cut in softly.

Her stomach flipped over and all of a sudden she didn't want to laugh any more. This felt dangerous. She couldn't cope with it. She didn't know the rules of the game and it made her feel scared. 'Stop it!'

'What?'

'You can't resist flirting, can you? Does anyone ever take you seriously?'

He said nothing—and it was immensely satisfying to feel back in control.

Jemima swallowed. 'Where was I?' she asked,

trying to recapture the light mood. 'Oh, yes, I heard the bit about my arriving late and leaving early. Not wanting to socialise—'

'You got it all,' Miles said, holding up his hand to stop her. 'I'm really sorry. I had no business talking about you like that.'

He seemed genuine. Jemima shrugged and turned back to her car. 'Don't worry about it.' His words had hurt, but not as much as he might imagine. She'd never valued the way she looked. How could she when she would always be in the shadow of a super-model sister. 'I know I don't fit into the Kingsley and Bressington image.'

'I was out of order.'

She turned in time to see Miles thrust an agitated hand through his dark hair. 'Your timekeeping is fine. You're always there by nine-thirty and don't leave until six. That's exactly what we asked for.'

'I did tell Amanda. It's because the boys need to be—'

'It's fine,' he cut her off firmly. 'Nine-thirty is fine.' He frowned and then asked, 'Will you be in on Monday?'

'No choice. I promised Amanda I'd stay for the duration. She thinks it's all good experience for me.' On Friday when she'd posted her time sheet back that had been a grim prospect, but it didn't feel so bad any more. 'Besides,' she added with a sudden grin, 'she told me on Friday afternoon how pleased you were with my work. Now, unless you were lying to her…'

His crack of laughter made her feel terrific. She didn't want to think why. She opened the car door.

'Jemima?'

She turned. 'Yes?'

'Why didn't you tell Rachel we'd met?'

Jemima smiled. 'Same reason you didn't, I imagine—just too complicated.'

'True.'

She climbed into the driver's seat. 'One or the other is going to need to ring Amanda, though. If we leave it to chance she's bound to say something to Rachel and then we'll look very stupid.'

'I'll do it.'

'What will you say?'

'Don't know.' Miles rested his hand on the car door, preventing her from closing it. 'The truth usually works best. Might have to be a little sparing with it, but basically I'll stick to the truth.'

Jemima laughed again and put her keys into the ignition. Miles took that as his cue to shut the car door and then he stepped back on the pavement, clearly waiting until she drove off. She just prayed that this was one of those occasions when her Volvo started without trouble.

Please, she murmured. *Just start*.

Somehow it wasn't a surprise when the engine turned over without firing up. Jemima closed her eyes and sent up a tiny arrow prayer, then tried the engine again.

Of course, it shouldn't matter at all that her car was failing in front of Miles Kingsley. It *didn't* matter. Of course it didn't. It was just…

If there was any justice in the world she'd have twisted the ignition key and her old Volvo would have risen to the occasion and purred away into the distance.

'Problems?'

Just life. *Her* life. She couldn't even make a stylish exit. Jemima pinned a smile on her face and wound down the window. 'It's a little temperamental. Sometimes is doesn't start straight away. I'll give it a little rest and try again in a minute.'

'Sounds like the battery's flat.'

Yep, it sounded like that to her. You didn't need to be a mechanic to know that the battery sounded as dead as a dodo. 'I'm sure it'll be fine. Don't bother waiting. If there's a problem I can ring for a taxi.'

'Try it again.'

It seemed he wasn't going anywhere. Jemima twisted the key again and the silence was deafening. Sometimes it helped if she pumped the accelerator, but mostly what helped was the downhill run she had from her house. Once it was going it was usually fine.

Of course, she could always suggest he gave her

a push. Sometimes that worked well… There was a part of her that wished she had the audacity to do it. The mental image of an impeccably dressed Miles Kingsley pushing a battered old Volvo had a certain appeal. But if it didn't work she'd be left blocking the road and, worse than that, her temporary boss would then get the opportunity to see how difficult she found reverse parking…

This was so mortifying, though why it felt so *particularly* mortifying she didn't know.

'It doesn't sound like it's going to work.'

'No.'

'Have you got any jump-leads?'

Now that would have been sensible. Jemima had a mental picture of the shelf in the utility room where she'd left them. *Why* hadn't she brought them? She always did if she was doing anything longer than the school run.

But tonight she'd been so late. That last little bit of wall in the bathroom had needed painting and it had been so tempting to finish before she went out. If she hadn't left it so late to get ready she probably wouldn't have tripped over the paint lid, wouldn't have needed to grab a shower and, therefore, wouldn't have forgotten the jump-leads. Strange how one seemingly innocuous decision could set you up for disaster.

'Unfortunately not,' she said, bravely climbing back out of the car. 'Have you?'

He shook his head.

Stupid question. Why would he have jump-leads in his car? Miles Kingsley probably drove a top of the range BMW or a flashy-looking Porsche. Jemima shivered as much from embarrassment as cold. What she really needed was Miles to go away and leave her to it.

Jemima looked back down the road towards her friend's flat. Perhaps Rachel had jump-leads? It didn't seem likely. She wasn't sure that Rachel knew how to open the bonnet of her car, but Alistair was the kind of man who would have jump-leads.

'Are you going to go back inside?' Miles asked, turning to follow her gaze.

Together they watched the bedroom curtains close. Jemima forced a smile. 'No. I can't face waiting for the AA to tow me home. I think I'll just ring for a taxi on my mobile and deal with it all in the morning. The boys aren't back until four. I've got plenty of time.'

It seemed like a great plan to her, but Miles didn't look convinced. 'Where do you live?'

'Harrow,' she said, turning back to look forlornly at her car. It was going to cost a lot of money to take a taxi, particularly at this time of night—even assuming she could find a driver who wanted to go that far out of central London.

'I'll give you a lift.'

Jemima whipped round to look at him. 'I—I couldn't ask you to do that.'

'You didn't.' Miles nodded at Alistair and Rachel's flat. 'They've gone to bed and I can't leave you waiting in the street for a taxi—'

'Your mother wouldn't like it,' Jemima quipped, unable to resist the thought that had popped into her head.

'You've got it.' He pulled his car keys from his jacket pocket.

Jemima hesitated.

'If I minded I wouldn't have offered. I'm staggeringly selfish. Consider it an opportunity for me to salve my conscience for having been so rude to you.' He started to walk back towards Alistair and Rachel's flat.

Why was he doing this? Driving her out to Harrow had to be the last thing he wanted to do. Hell, this was so embarrassing. She wanted to curl up in a ball and howl, only that wasn't an option.

With one last look at her Volvo, Jemima followed him back along the pavement. Perhaps she should just ring the AA? But they'd take a while to get to her and Miles would probably insist on waiting with her. So that would be equally embarrassing—and the prospect of ringing the AA for the third time in six months *really* didn't appeal. They'd probably be irritated because it was palpably obvious she needed to do something about replacing the car. It was dying—and she knew it.

Jemima bit her lip and tried to decide what was the least embarrassing option open to her. In her next life, she decided, this kind of thing was not going to be allowed to happen. She was going to be effortlessly elegant, thin, possibly blonde…

'Coming?'

'Yes.'

Miles's car was showroom perfect—as she'd known it would be. It was also old—*very* old—and she hadn't expected that. Cars weren't high on her list of interesting things, but for this particular model she might make an exception. It was truly a classic.

'It's a 1962 Bristol 407,' Miles said, watching her. 'Don't say it…'

She looked up questioningly.

'I know.' His mouth twisted into a wry smile. 'The ultimate Boy's Own accessory.'

Now that he said it… Jemima smiled. 'It's even older than my car.'

Miles opened the passenger door. 'But greater loved.'

Despite everything she felt a bubble of laughter start somewhere in the pit of her stomach. Being with Miles was an exhilarating experience, Jemima thought as his Bristol 407 pulled away from the kerb. Before the boys, before Russell…before life had robbed her of optimism…she might have been tempted by him. It felt exciting being with someone like him, as though anything could happen and probably would.

She smiled in the darkness. Even before the boys, Miles would never have been seriously interested in a woman like her. Or even un-seriously, since that appeared to be all he did. He was the kind of man Verity dated. They'd look great together...

But even Verity hoped she'd meet someone one day who'd be able to see beneath the beautiful veneer and love her. Just her. It was strange that Miles was so adamant he'd never marry. Most people hoped that one day they might find someone to share their life with. *Didn't they?* Jemima glanced across at his handsome profile. It was unusual not to want to find a soul mate. Didn't he feel a need to be loved and share his life with someone?

'Why are you so negative towards marriage?' she asked suddenly.

He turned his head to look at her, before refocusing on the road. 'Did it show? I was making a special effort to be positive.'

Jemima laughed. 'I know. I heard the instruction, remember. I'm "brittle".'

She felt his smile. 'And are you?' He glanced across at her.

Yes. No. No one ever asked her that outright. She'd spoken without thinking and she didn't know how to answer him. She was just 'poor Jemima'. The lame duck that everyone had to rally around. 'You tell me.'

'Evasion,' he said softly, his eyes still on the road.

Jemima took a sharp intake of breath. Was she 'brittle'? Surely she was stronger than that? She was holding it together, doing really well under the circumstances. She sighed. 'I think I'm walking wounded.'

He looked at her and smiled and, all of a sudden, it didn't seem to matter any more what people were saying and thinking about her. The air in the confines of the small car seemed rarefied and she felt light-headed.

Jemima looked down at her hands, white against the dark linen of her dress. She wasn't good at this one-to-one with an attractive man. She didn't understand how the game went.

And he was attractive, that small voice whispered. Very. She'd known that since her first morning at Kingsley and Bressington. Miles Kingsley was scarily sexy—and way, way out of her league. She sighed and gave a tentative smile. 'I'm trying to support Rachel…but I just can't summon up any enthusiasm for confetti and white ribbon. It doesn't seem particularly relevant to anything any more.'

Miles looked across with another smile. It was perfect. Warm, but not pitying. It was like a shot of whisky—supremely comforting.

'I feel guilty, though,' she continued, hurriedly looking away. 'Rachel was my bridesmaid and she put in more effort than I'm doing. We spent hours poring over magazines. We even made an ideas scrapbook. How sad was that?'

She heard his smile rather than saw it. It was in his voice. 'Rachel must have known you were going to find it difficult when she asked you to be her bridesmaid.'

'I suppose.'

'In fact, are you a bridesmaid?' Miles looked at her. 'Do you return to virginal status after a divorce or do you become a matron of honour?'

Jemima felt another laugh well up inside her. 'That's your problem. You've got to do the speech.'

'Thanks for that!'

She slipped her foot out of her flat pump and rubbed the back of her right heel with her toes. 'It's probably better to make me a "bridesmaid" since Russell's going to be at the wedding.'

'Your ex?'

She nodded. 'It's bad enough I'm still using his name. We've been divorced just over a year and were separated for eighteen months before that.'

'So why do you?' he asked, his hands moving easily on the steering wheel.

'It seemed simpler to have the same name as my boys. You know, less confusing at the school gate.'

He nodded his understanding, but she wasn't

sure whether he thought it a good enough reason. She wasn't sure whether it was either. 'Anyway, Alistair and Rachel asked if I'd mind if they asked him. Rachel's known him since university...' Jemima drew a breath. 'So he's coming...with Stefanie.'

'Couldn't you have said you did mind?'

She gave a hard laugh. 'I could, but then Russell would have known I was uncomfortable about him being there...and I couldn't have that. In fact, everyone would have known I'd said I minded and then they'd have felt sorry for me.' She turned to look at him. 'I've had enough of that. I must have heard every possible connotation of "poor Jemima" going.'

'It's a tough deal to be bringing up two children on your own.'

'Russell helps. He's really good.' A familiar sense of gloom spread through her body. She hated the way everyone said that. What was so good about walking out on your family? 'And he's great with the boys. Spends as much time with them as he can.'

It was me he left. That small voice bit into her self-esteem. Russell had enjoyed everything about his life—but *her.* She wasn't about to tell Miles that. She hadn't told anyone how...destroyed she felt by that. The person who had promised to love her until she died had taken a sledgehammer and smashed her to smithereens. *How did you stick yourself back together after that?*

'It's not the same though, is it?' Miles indicated to move lanes. 'The ultimate responsibility is yours. I imagine it's the same difference as running a company and being employed by one. The emotional investment is completely different.'

Put like that her sense of crushing responsibility seemed entirely reasonable. She turned slightly in her chair. 'So, what's your excuse? Why are you so lacking in enthusiasm about marriage? You didn't say.'

Miles glanced across at her. 'I've got no problem with the ideal; it's just I don't believe it's achievable. Two people in a monogamous relationship which lasts fifty years plus…?' He shook his head.

'People have done it.'

'Perhaps. I don't know.' He smiled. 'People change. Circumstances certainly do. Apart from anything else, we all live a great deal longer now and I'm not convinced it's possible to find one person who will be a perfect fit for an entire lifetime.'

Jemima thought for a moment. What he said sounded plausible—but *bleak*. Did he really believe that? It sounded like something Hermione Kingsley might say in one of her strident columns. 'Maybe not "perfect", not all the time…but don't you think it's possible to evolve together? If you value what you have enough…' That was what she believed.

'Wouldn't it be simpler to accept that one person might be right for a period of your life, and then someone quite different for a different period?'

No. It was such a cold and isolated way of living. She couldn't accept that. Jemima frowned. 'What about children? Don't you believe they do better with stability?'

'Ah.'

She looked at him curiously.

'Now you've found the rub to my argument. In many ways I had a great childhood. Materially privileged, great schools…' Miles broke off and glanced across at her. 'You're going to need to start directing me on where I should be going.'

'Oh.' Jemima thrust her foot back in her shoe. 'Straight on here. Take the third exit at the next roundabout. We're nearly there.'

Miles glanced across at her and his eyes crinkled. 'The trouble with my argument is that I know I wasn't very interested in my mother's principles as a child.' He focused back on the road. 'It was all fine, no doubt, but I desperately wanted to have a dad. Of course, in my case, it was all a little extreme.'

'A little,' Jemima agreed, wondering how difficult it had been for him to have grown up with a mother who was so public about the circumstances of his unconventional conception.

He paused while he negotiated the roundabout.

'I wonder… If I'd been conceived in a more usual way…'

'Yes?'

'I don't think I'd have been remotely concerned about my parents' marital happiness. I think I'd have simply been happy to have someone on hand to play cricket with and produce on Parents Day.'

Jemima felt a rumble of laughter. 'That does rather blow your life plan out of the water.'

'Only if I have children.' His eyes flicked across at her. 'It's not my intention. I like things exactly as they are. Why change it?'

No children. Ever. Miles might be right in his assessment of the realities of modern day living, but she preferred to believe it was possible to spend a lifetime loving one person. Hope in the face of experience. 'It's the third turning on the right.'

'This one?'

'That's it,' she said, and a few seconds later, 'The one with the burgundy door.'

They pulled up outside and Jemima felt conscious of the peeling paintwork and the generally unkempt appearance. 'Thanks. I appreciate you bringing me home,' she said awkwardly.

'It's no problem.'

All at once she felt as if she was seventeen again, coming home after a date. Jemima bent to pick up her handbag, not quite sure what she should do now. It felt *awkward*. Should she ask him in for coffee? Or not? What was the correct thing to do when your friend's best man was also your temporary boss?

But he had gone out of his way and driven her home…

And he could always say no… Probably would.

Take a deep breath and ask him.

It was just coffee.

In the end she took it in a rush. 'Do you want a coffee before you drive back?'

CHAPTER FOUR

IT WASN'T as though asking Miles in for coffee would turn this evening into any kind of a romantic interlude. It was nothing more than common courtesy.

Jemima gritted her teeth and waited for his answer—the inevitable no. Of course, he'd say no. It was a long way back into central London—assuming, of course, Miles lived in central London. He might not. He might live somewhere closer, like Pinner or Ruislip…

'Coffee would be great.'

Jemima's eyes widened in shock. 'R-right.' *Coffee was easy. She could do coffee.*

'It's not as though I've anywhere I need to be.' Miles smiled and her stomach flipped over like a pancake. Whoever his mystery sperm donor had been, he'd donated some seriously good genes to the pot.

His smile made her forget she was the mother

of two boys, forget that her Victorian semi needed a new roof, forget that her bedroom had a scary damp patch in the corner by the window. All these things seemed to vaporise and she was left with a breathless excitement.

'That's not what you told Rachel,' she managed.

'Implied,' Miles corrected. 'Like you, there's only so much confetti and white ribbon I can stomach. Once you'd made your break for freedom it seemed sensible to follow on behind you. Good job, too, since it's given me the opportunity to play Sir Galahad.'

Jemima felt for the door handle.

'Hang on. I'll help you out,' he said, climbing out his side and walking round.

Jemima couldn't remember the last time a man had opened a car door for her. Miles made it seem such a natural, contemporary thing to do. 'Thanks,' she said as he shut the passenger door.

'It's a shame to have to go back in to town tomorrow, though. It's going to take up most of your Sunday.'

She shrugged. 'It doesn't matter.'

Miles's eyes narrowed astutely, but he didn't say anything. Jemima wondered what he was thinking. He couldn't possibly understand how lonely she felt on the weekends her boys were with Russell. It was like an ache. She was always wondering where they were, what they were doing. The days stretched out endlessly and, despite the hundred and one jobs she had to do, she found she was listless.

Jemima glanced up at the peeling paintwork on the front door and wished she'd done something about that on one of her 'weekends'. 'It's a work in progress,' she cautioned.

'What?'

'The h-house,' she clarified, searching for her keys. 'It's a bit of a mess.'

'You're renovating it, aren't you?'

'Well, that was the plan,' she agreed, fitting the key into the lock. 'Progress is a bit slow.' That was a bit of an understatement. If it wasn't for the generosity of her family, it would have all but ground to a halt.

'I imagine it's difficult with children around,' Miles said neutrally.

Jemima glanced across at him in the dark. It *was* difficult with the children around, but there was so much more to it than that. More even than the lack of money. It was surprisingly difficult without someone to bounce ideas off. Every decision seemed momentous. Even choosing tiles for the bathroom.

She knew, of course, that against the wider context of world poverty and social injustice how she decorated her bathroom didn't rate as anything more than a dot. Nevertheless it felt important.

The door opened on to the original Minton tiled floor and Jemima stepped inside.

'The floor's great,' Miles observed. 'You were lucky to find a place where it's in such good condition.'

'I know. It's one of the reasons we bought it. That and the fact there's a good primary school at the end of the road,' she added.

'We?'

'Russell and I. He was really great about us having the house when he left,' Jemima said with determined cheerfulness. 'He didn't want the boys to have to move. You know, Ben was settled in school and Sam had only just had his bedroom decorated…'

She was rambling. She knew she was. Jemima bit her lip and made a conscious decision to stop. Miles wouldn't be interested.

'Is he going to deal with the roof?'

Jemima turned back to look at him, her eyes wide with surprise. 'Of course not. It's my responsibility now.'

No one had ever asked anything like that before. It made such a change for someone not to be impressed at how 'great' Russell was being about everything. She was just a little tired of being grateful to the man who had torn her family apart for no other reason than that he'd felt bored.

'How far have you got with everything else?' Miles asked, his shoes loud on the tiled floor.

Jemima pulled a face and switched on the light further down the hall. 'See for yourself.'

Miles said nothing. He didn't need to. Jemima was acutely aware of how much still needed to be done. There was still painted woodchip paper in the hallway and even gloss paint over what she was sure would be original tiles in the fireplace in the sitting room.

'It's coming on,' she said bravely. 'The kitchen is basically finished and I've just had a new bathroom fitted in one of the upstairs bedrooms. Maybe I'll think about re-roofing the house next.'

If she won the lottery, she added silently. Or accepted yet more help from her family.

This was embarrassing. Why the blazes had she asked him in for coffee? Jemima caught sight of herself in the hall mirror and ran a despairing hand through her red curls. She looked a mess too. Like some kind of Muppet.

They walked through to the kitchen, with its sleek maple units and dark worktops. Her eyes instinctively turned to the one thing that was different—the small puddle on the central island. Her eyes moved upwards to take in the damp stain on the papered ceiling and she watched a single drip fall down. 'Oh—'

'Damn,' Miles finished for her.

'Something like that,' she agreed, dropping her handbag. For a moment Jemima couldn't decide what to do and then she hurried into the redundant bathroom and returned with a red plastic bucket. *Perfect. Just perfect.* First the car, now this. 'Why does this always happen to me? I ricochet from one disaster to another.'

'It happens to everyone,' Miles replied with infuriating calmness. He slipped off his jacket and threw it carelessly across one of the high bar stools. 'It's one of the joys of owning property, but it's usually better than it looks.'

Jemima plonked the bucket on top of the worktop and then searched for some kitchen towel to wipe up the water already there. 'In my experience, it's almost always worse,' she muttered.

He didn't seem to be listening. His eyes were fixed on the stain on the ceiling. 'Have you got something sharp to make a hole? I reckon you ought to let the water out and contain the damage.'

'Pardon?'

'It looks like it's collecting up there. Water always finds a level,' he explained patiently. 'It'll spread and become more of a problem if you leave it until you can get hold of a plumber.'

Spread. Just great. Of course, she knew water always found its own level—it was just she hadn't connected that fact with a leaking ceiling. Jemima went back out to the old bathroom and rummaged through her tool box. She picked out a bradawl. It probably had a very specific use in the hands of an expert, but it also looked like the kind of thing that would be excellent for making a hole in a papered ceiling.

'Do you want me to do it?' Miles asked as she returned.

'No.' Jemima slipped off her shoes and climbed on to the central island. 'If there's got to be a hole in my ceiling, I'll do it.'

'Fair enough.'

His voice was so bland that she looked down at him. 'I know your mother would be proud,' she said.

Miles laughed.

'This isn't funny.'

'It's not bad from where I'm standing.'

Jemima ignored him, shut her eyes and pushed hard. It took a fairly stiff twist before she managed to make a hole. Almost immediately, water started to trickle down into the bucket below. With gritted teeth, she used the bradawl to make the hole bigger.

'That'll do it.'

'It's wrecked the ceiling paper,' Jemima observed as she looked at her handiwork, feeling a sudden unexpected desire to cry. She really didn't want to do *that* in front of Miles. It would be the final indignity and he must already think she was a walking disaster area.

'That's cheap to sort.'

She climbed down and drew an irritated hand

across her eyes. What was the matter with her? She didn't usually allow the house to get her down. She only felt like crying because she was so tired. In the morning this would all look so much better…

'It's slowing down.'

'Is it?' Jemima asked doubtfully, looking back up at the damp mess of her ceiling.

'I know it looks like a lot of water at the moment, but I'm fairly sure it's not going to be a major problem. How long ago did you have your bathroom fitted?'

'The plumber finished a couple of days ago.' She couldn't believe it! Two days. *Damn it!* It just wasn't fair…

'Then it's probably no more serious than he dislodged something while he was doing the job. Give him a ring on Monday.'

'And you're the expert?' Jemima said, finally irritated by his…*smug* calmness. Everybody was always so good at making light of problems that weren't their own.

'Not specifically in plumbing, but in renovating houses.' His blue eyes glinted as though he knew exactly what she was thinking. 'I'm on my sixth.'

'Sixth?'

'House,' he said with a smile. 'In ten years. Do you want to check upstairs? I doubt there'll be anything to see, but you ought to look.'

She hated that he was right. She should have

thought of that for herself. Jemima put the bradawl down on the worktop and padded barefoot across the kitchen and up the stairs. The bathroom looked as chaotic as she'd left it. The welkin blue foot-prints were still on the vinyl floor waiting to be cleared up, but there was no sign of any leak.

She took a deep breath and returned to the kitchen.

Miles looked up as she walked in. 'Well?'

'Nothing.' She glanced up at the ceiling. 'You wouldn't know anything had happened.'

He smiled, the blue eyes crinkling at the edges. 'That's good. It's unlikely to be an expensive job. So, what about that coffee?'

Jemima found she automatically turned towards the kettle. She filled it with water and flicked the switch before asking curiously, 'Do you really renovate houses? I mean personally?'

His smile intensified. 'You really don't think a lot of me, do you, Ms Chadwick?'

'Apart from the dandelion thing, I haven't thought about you at all,' she responded quickly. More reflex action than anything else, but as soon as the words had left her mouth she wished she hadn't said them. The poor guy had given her a lift home, had stayed while she sorted out the latest disaster to hit her life…

She glanced across at him to find he was laughing. 'I'm sorry—that was rude.'

'Why do you find it surprising I renovate houses? It can be very profitable.'

She looked over her shoulder to find he'd perched comfortably on one of the high bar stools. He might be wearing jeans, but they weren't the kind she recognised and they certainly hadn't come from the high street. 'Well…' She frowned.

'Go on, I can take it.'

Jemima looked across at him and smiled in defeat. 'You don't exactly come across as a handyman. I can't imagine you spending hours stripping wallpaper or tiling.'

Miles laughed. 'I'm not bad, but I tend to buy in these days, more than do it myself.'

'Nice to have the choice.'

'That's what I think,' he agreed with a smile and her stomach flipped. The realisation hit her that she liked being with him. So often when she was talking to other people she felt as if she was playing tennis by herself, but with Miles every ball came back with spin. It felt a little dangerous, certainly exciting.

Jemima turned away and put a teaspoon of coffee granules into a mug. 'Is instant okay?'

'Fine.'

He even managed to make that sound as though he meant it. Kingsley and Bressington had beautiful coffee—expensive, rich and freshly ground. Jemima straightened her shoulders and tried not to think about it. 'You do know black coffee stains your teeth?'

'So I'm told.'

Jemima felt her mouth curve into a smile. She almost didn't mind about the leak. How did Miles *do* that? In the space of one evening he'd gone from a temporary boss she didn't much like to someone who felt like a friend. Almost. He was too unsettling to be something as comfortable as a friend.

She put milk in her own coffee, followed by a sweetener, before she turned round to find he was watching her. She passed him his coffee with a hand that shook slightly.

'Thanks.'

Miles made her feel self-conscious. It was something in his expression. Something she didn't quite understand. Something that made her breath shallow and her voice sound as though it were catching on cobwebs.

'I—I did wonder whether I could take that out,' Jemima said, looking at the old chimney-breast, 'and make a big family room in here.'

'Nice idea, but it'll be too expensive—'

'Oh, not now. Later on. When I've got a better job than working as your temporary secretary.' She paused to sip her coffee and watched him over the top of her mug. His eyes had started to laugh again and she felt her own mouth curve in response. It was automatic. An involuntary response. He made her feel alive and, she realised with a shock, she hadn't felt like that in months. Perhaps years. There was always so much to do. So many responsibilities. Most of the time she just felt tired.

But this evening…

With Miles…

'It's a phenomenally expensive thing to do. That chimney stack goes up three floors and you'd have to take it out all the way up. You'd be better off putting a conservatory type extension out the side here.' He stood up and walked over to the window.

It gave Jemima a perfect view of how fantastically he filled his designer jeans. In a formal suit he looked intimidating; in more casual clothes it was far worse. You could really see how muscular his thighs were and how tight his buttocks. She swallowed.

What was happening to her? *Never* in her entire life had she thought about a man the way she was thinking about this one. She'd always gone for the safe option. She wasn't the kind of girl who'd ever have coped well with the style of casual dating Miles favoured. She thought about consequences and weighed every decision she made carefully. That was *who* she was. It was ingrained in her personality as though it were carved there.

And Miles was who he was. Different from her. Shaped by his background as certainly as she'd been by her own.

Even if Miles were to look up and notice her…
Jemima smiled even at the possibility of the possibility. She'd be terrified. Totally and utterly terrified.

Jemima sipped her coffee to hide her face. Miles seemed to have the uncanny knack of being able to read her mind and it wouldn't do for him to get an inkling of where her thoughts were taking her now.

He turned to look at her. 'If you've got the space to push the house out sideways it would link the kitchen and breakfast room together, besides bringing in so much more light. I've seen it done and it looks incredible.'

'You really do know about this renovation thing, don't you?'

His mouth pulled into a crooked smile. 'Frustrated designer.'

'Really?' Jemima wouldn't have thought he'd been frustrated in anything he wanted to do. He had the aura of a man who habitually succeeded in everything. It was interesting to think he might have been thwarted in something. Unbelievable, really.

He walked back towards her. 'I did my degree in Industrial Design.'

'How come you went into public relations?' Jemima asked, genuinely curious.

Miles shrugged. 'Seemed sensible at the time.'

'No, really,' she prompted. Miles didn't easily

talk about himself, it seemed. He either turned the conversation or he gave a flip answer which made everyone laugh and forget about all about the question they'd asked. Was that a conscious technique he used? Her eyes narrowed astutely. 'I'd like to know.'

He appeared to hesitate for a moment and then he shrugged. It was a kind of victory. 'Oh, I gave design a chance. I set up a company out of a caravan in the Lake District with a friend from university. Dan and I came up with some fantastic ideas, but not surprisingly found it difficult to get anyone to take us seriously.'

He still smiled, but he seemed more guarded. She sensed he wasn't used to failure and he didn't speak about it easily.

'We were both twenty-two and very inexperienced. Not to mention that I came with an image that didn't inspire much confidence in the design world.' He shrugged again. 'In the end Dan decided he needed to eat and the idea folded.'

'That's a shame.'

Miles smiled. 'I couldn't blame him for that. I had an allowance paid into my bank account every month. Dan was on his own.'

Miles sounded as if he really minded. It surprised her. She'd been silly to think he was invincible and impenetrable to hurt—no one was. 'And then?' she asked after a moment.

'Then I sold my soul to the devil.' He smiled. 'Public relations was an obvious choice for someone with my background. I've been dealing with the media since I was in my mother's womb.'

She wasn't sure what to say. 'You're good at it.'

The blue of his eyes intensified as the laughter returned. 'Professional lying…?'

Jemima bit her lip. 'Sorry about that.'

'Don't apologise. I deserved it.'

'Yes, you did,' she said, cradling her hands around her mug. 'I wonder what Amanda will make of us not saying anything. It would have been much simpler to own up that we'd already met.'

He shook his head. 'I'd never have lived it down. Alistair would never have let me forget it.'

Miles watched as Jemima uncurled her hands from her mug. She really did have beautiful hands. They didn't need long nails and brightly coloured varnish. She looked fresh…and real. That was it. It had been a long time, he realised with a pang, since he'd spent any time with a woman who hadn't dressed to impress him. Or if not him specifically, men in general.

Jemima simply didn't care. Miles smiled, watching the way she was concentrating on the warmth her mug gave off. If anything she was reserving judgement on whether she liked him. That really did make a change.

Normally he was the centre of attention. He

knew that he had to do the barest minimum to get a woman to accept a dinner invitation—assuming she was single and heterosexual. But Jemima…

He rather fancied he'd be whistling in the wind if he tried to get her to take him seriously. She was more concerned about her ceiling and what that might mean to her bank balance. He watched as she looked up at it and he could almost read the thoughts passing through her head.

Then she smiled at him, quite suddenly, and he felt the air freeze around him.

'It seems to be stopping. There's no point standing about in here. It's all a bit depressing. Let's go into the sitting room.'

'Okay,' he said, picking up his jacket.

She led the way back into the hall and along to the main reception room. 'Of course, it's a bit depressing in here too. Every time I sit in here I'm reminded of how much there is to do.'

The sitting room was exactly as he'd expected it would be. He'd seen many Victorian semis which had been 'improved' in just such a way during the sixties and seventies. The ceiling was covered with thick Artex, which would be both expensive and messy to remove, the walls were painted woodchip and the carpet was predominantly brown with overblown yellow roses on it.

Jemima followed the line of his gaze. 'My son thinks they look like cabbages.'

'It's all cosmetic stuff. Great the fireplace surround has survived.'

'Yes,' she agreed, curling up in one of the comfortable sofas like a kitten. 'It's a shame about the tiles.'

'You should be able to get the paint off. It would have been a disaster if they'd been chipped off.' Miles took the sofa opposite. He scarcely knew Jemima—didn't know Russell at all—but he felt a spurt of anger when he thought of the situation she'd been left in. The house had enormous potential, but it was a money pit.

It was a wonder she hadn't cried when she came home to discover she'd taken two steps forward and one back. It must be heartbreaking. And she'd faced it all with determination and a toss of that incredible red hair. It was courage…and he admired it.

He smiled as he thought of her, barefooted, bradawl in hand. Unconsciously sexy. It seemed he'd often thought that about her tonight. She was a woman without artifice—and he'd begun to think they didn't exist.

Miles sipped his coffee, watching her. Jemima had the most amazing skin. It was clear, almost translucent, with a smattering of freckles across her nose. Every other woman he knew would have covered them up with some magic concoction from Estée Lauder. But not Jemima…

Sun-kissed. *Sexy*. She had no idea how much he wanted to kiss her right now. He smiled. Probably just as well.

His eyes followed the line of the mantelpiece. There were photographs of two boys, both dark-haired. Handsome. The elder had serious green eyes, very like his mother's. The younger was full of fun. He looked uncomplicated, as though life didn't trouble him much.

Jemima's voice cut in on his thoughts. 'The photographer said "sausages".'

'Pardon?'

She nodded at the photographs. 'That's why he's laughing. Apparently it's very funny when you're five.'

'Which is which?' Miles asked, turning back to look at her.

'Ben is the elder. He's eight. Sam is five.'

Miles stood up and walked over to have a closer look. He had to keep remembering Jemima Chadwick was a single mum—with responsibilities. It put her firmly out of bounds. If a single mum was in the market for a no-strings relationship she shouldn't be.

Personal freedom was all well and good, but he knew first hand how it felt to be dragged through a series of short-term father-son relationships. How it felt to be without a secure base. Never quite knowing which 'special friend' his mother would have introduced into his home each holiday.

Occasionally, very occasionally, he'd like one or another, but their involvement in his life had always been brief. Miles didn't consider he had much of a code of honour, but, for what it was worth, this was his. He'd *never* let himself get involved with a woman who had children. It wasn't fair on the children.

Miles picked up the photograph of the elder child. Ben, wasn't it? He looked like a sensitive boy. Intelligent.

Not unlike how he'd looked as a child, he thought, taking in the guarded expression. Ben would find his father leaving him difficult to deal with. He knew it as certainly as if he'd been told. It was a betrayal, and betrayal dug deep. How could a child be expected to understand the full ramifications of adult emotions? The whys and the wherefores?

Even now, as an adult himself, he didn't really understand it all. No doubt a psychoanalyst would have a field day if he allowed them to delve into his motivations. He put the picture of Ben back down on the mantelpiece.

However tempted he might be, Jemima Chadwick would remain unkissed. His eyes followed along the mantelpiece and he gave a cursory glance at the next cluster of photographs. Lots of smiling groups—more snapshots than formal portraiture. Presumably they were of extended family? Parents?

And...

He didn't quite believe what he was seeing. He looked closer, then over his shoulder. 'You know Verity Hunt?'

Was it his imagination or did Jemima curl up more tightly on the sofa? 'She's my sister.'

Verity Hunt? Jemima's sister? Miles looked again at the photograph, almost prepared to disbelieve her.

'Younger sister,' Jemima continued, as though it were nothing out of the ordinary. 'Imogen is the eldest. She's a homeopathic vet. Married, three children, three ponies, a house in Cheshire and a Danish au pair.'

'Sounds perfect,' Miles managed neutrally.

'I don't know about perfect, but it's a great place to go during the summer. She takes us in each year for a holiday. I've promised the boys we'll spend at least a week with them before they go back to school in September.'

Miles took a moment to look more closely at the picture of Imogen and her family. Of the two sisters, she was the most like Jemima, but she lacked the stunning hair. In any other circumstances her strawberry-blonde would have been dramatic. Against Jemima's vibrant mane it looked washed out and colourless.

Verity was completely different again. She had

a gamine look and a smooth shining curtain of carefully highlighted chestnut hair.

Jemima pulled her legs in closer. 'Do you know Verity?'

'No.' He crossed back to the sofa and sat down. 'At least I've met her at a couple of parties, but I can't say I know her. We certainly don't handle her PR…but you must know that.'

It wasn't appropriate to say, but what he remembered most about Verity was that he'd thought her less beautiful than her photographs—something that wasn't uncommon with models. They had amazing bone structure and the camera loved them, but that didn't necessarily translate into a real beauty. Not the kind you wanted to find curled up under your duvet, anyway.

Nevertheless, she must be a difficult act to live up to. The homeopathic vet too. How hard was it to see your life disintegrating around you when your siblings were living the dream?

'I wondered whether you might know her. We don't look similar. Obviously.' Jemima smiled and he thought she looked sad. 'She's lovely. Both my sisters are.'

If Verity Hunt was so lovely, the question that begged to be asked was—why didn't she help with re-roofing the house? The sister with the three ponies and the Danish au pair didn't look like she was strapped for cash either.

Miles glanced across at Jemima. There was no
way he could ask her that. It would be treading on
far too personal ground. Her whole body language
had mutated from that of a kitten to something
entirely more wary.

'Verity lives abroad for most of the year,'
Jemima continued tonelessly. 'She has a flat in
Manhattan.' Then she shook her head. 'No, that's
wrong. It's an *apartment*. I never remember to call
it that. She also has a smaller place in Milan. It's
tiny, but it has the most stunning roof ter-
race leading off the kitchen. She had an architect
who—'

The telephone rang.

Jemima broke off and looked at her watch. Immediately her face paled and she threw the cushion
on the floor. '*Oh, God*, I hope the boys…'

CHAPTER FIVE

MILES pulled himself forward on the sofa, draining the last of his coffee. It was too late for someone to be calling casually—well past midnight. Jemima was probably right to suspect the worst.

'Hello.'

There was a short silence. Miles put his mug down on the low 'apprentice' chest which served as a coffee table. He sat poised, ready to leave or to help, whatever was the most appropriate.

Jemima tucked her hair behind her ear. 'I've been out for dinner.' Another pause while the person on the other end spoke and then, 'I must have had my mobile switched off. I'm sorry. What's happened? Are the boys okay?'

It didn't take any imagination to realise she must be talking to the absent Russell. So why was she apologising to him? What for? It was entirely within her rights to turn her mobile on or off as she saw fit. And none of her ex-husband's business any more where she was.

Miles found himself wondering what Russell Chadwick would be like. What kind of man would Jemima have married? And what kind of man, for that matter, would walk away from a woman like Jemima?

Miles watched as Jemima's face took on an expression of intense worry. *Something had happened to one of her boys*. He felt the low kick of dread as he observed the change in her. Her knuckles were white from the fierce hold she had on the receiver and there were deep frown lines in the centre of her forehead.

In a way he couldn't possibly explain, she suddenly seemed more beautiful. There was a luminosity to her that froze his breath. Just for a moment. Perhaps because he'd never seen what selfless love really looked like on a person.

Jemima would do anything, brave anything, for the people she loved deeply. It was written across her face. In his entire thirty-six years he wasn't sure he'd ever witnessed that kind of love. It was…awe-inspiring. And, in a strange way, it made him feel cheated. There was no one anywhere on earth who had ever felt that kind of love for him. Certainly not his mother. Hermione had her passions, but they'd never been centred around her only son. Currently she was in the Himalayas researching a new book and he doubted she would return for anything less than the news of his death.

Ben and Sam were lucky. They might never realise quite how much.

'I can't. The car's broken down.' Jemima glanced up at the clock. 'Perhaps I can call a cab…'

Miles spoke quietly. 'Where do you need to go?' Whatever it was that had happened, he couldn't drive away into the distance and leave her to deal with it alone. That was impossible. 'Can I help?'

Jemima pulled an agitated hand through her curls and stared at him as though she wasn't sure what she should say. 'Miles, I don't—' Then she broke off, clearly listening to her ex-husband on the other end of the phone.

Miles stood up, waiting.

She glanced across at him, then away, speaking into the phone. 'It's a friend. Hang on a second.' Jemima turned her incredible eyes, now full of worry, back towards him. 'It's Sam. My youngest. He's been sick and wants to come home.'

Miles felt his muscles relax. *Sick.* Nothing too serious, then. Just a little boy who would rather be with his mother. He could remember that feeling. Only his mother had been too busy to stay at home and nurse him. Whereas Jemima…

There was no question but that she'd move heaven and earth to make things right for her son.

However awkward she might find accepting another favour from him, Miles knew that she'd do it. And, strangely, there was no doubt that he'd do what he could to help.

Miles felt the stirrings of a smile. *What exactly was he getting himself into?* Somewhere up there someone clearly had an acute sense of humour, he thought as he experienced a momentary pang at the prospect of his precious Bristol 407 carrying a child who might well vomit.

'Do you need to go and fetch him?' he asked quietly.

'Ben's asleep and Russell doesn't want to wake—'

'Tell him we're on our way.' Miles didn't wait to hear what Jemima had to say. He shrugged on his jacket, catching only the edge of her smile. It was still enough to blow him away.

He was going to have to watch it. She was the kind of woman who might well get under your skin and stay there.

Jemima spoke into the receiver. 'Russell, I'm coming now. Tell Sam. Fifteen minutes and I'll be there.' She put the phone back into its cradle. 'Are you sure? I'm so sorry.'

'Don't waste time.' Miles smiled at her. He didn't want her gratitude. It seemed to him she'd spent a surfeit of her time being grateful to other people who may or may not deserve it. And he genuinely wanted to help her. He'd caught only the slightest glimpse of what her life was like...and it was the least he could do.

'No. I'll...' She tucked her hair behind her ears again in a nervous gesture. 'Right, I'd better fetch an old ice cream tub in case he feels unwell in the car...'

As she disappeared into the kitchen Miles thrust a hand through his hair. *Old ice cream tub?* Alistair wouldn't believe the way his evening was panning out, even if he told him—and he'd absolutely no intention of ever doing that.

Miles waited in the hall as Jemima flew past him.

'I'm going to grab the duvet off Sam's bed. I won't be a second.' She turned at the top of the stairs, stopping halfway up to say, 'Stuff it! I've left the ice cream tub on the island in the kitchen. Could you—'

'I'll fetch it. Get the duvet.'

Another first. Miles couldn't remember ever having spent the evening with a woman who'd ended up thinking absolutely nothing about him. Her attention was entirely focused on her son. Jemima would probably have driven off with the devil incarnate if it would have got her to Sam quickly. He admired her for that.

Miles smiled and walked through to the kitchen. He picked up the empty tub and pulled a face, hoping it hadn't been used for this particular purpose before and wouldn't be this time either. Beside the tub there was a small jar of Calpol. Without reading the label it looked medicinal, so he picked it up as well.

He came back into the hallway as Jemima was hurrying down the stairs with a duvet wrapped into a tight roll under one arm. She'd grabbed a pale green cardigan in soft angora. She looked...charming. Unconsciously charming. He cleared his throat. 'Do you want this?' he asked, holding up the bottle.

'Yes. Thanks. It's liquid paracetamol.' Jemima picked her handbag up from the hall chair. 'It's great for bringing temperatures down. Of course, it'll be no good if Sam's actually being sick...'

Miles held out the ice cream tub, trying not to think about that.

'It's okay. It's got a lid,' she said with a sudden smile, obviously able to read his expression.

The green wool of her cardigan intensified the colour of her eyes. He felt his mouth curve in an answering smile. 'Don't say it.' He stopped her, taking the duvet off her and giving her the tub. 'I don't want to know. That's advanced parenting and I'm strictly the chauffeur.'

Her smile widened. 'You know, I'm really grateful—'

He gave her a gentle push in the small of her back. 'Just go.'

She was lovely. If anyone had told him at the start of the evening he'd be driving through Harrow in the early hours of the morning to collect a sick child for his temporary secretary, he wouldn't have believed it. Miles glanced across at Jemima's profile. It felt right, though.

He wouldn't swap his life with hers for anything. She carried such responsibilities. Where in all of it was time for herself? Did she ever have a moment where she could think about absolutely nothing but herself and what she wanted? Somehow he doubted it and he wished…

Jemima looked across at him. 'What?'

Miles focused back on the road. He couldn't put words on what he was thinking. He didn't really understand what they were himself. 'Where now?'

'Take the second left at the next roundabout and follow the road on. There are a couple of T-junctions, but you need to keep going straight.'

'Okay.' There was silence for a few moments. Miles concentrated on the road, but was acutely aware of Jemima sitting beside him. Every now and again she shifted slightly in her seat, or brushed her hair away from her face. Small, totally insignificant movements, but for some reason he was aware of them.

He swallowed and searched for something to say. *That was a first too.* Not since he was thirteen had he struggled for something to say to a member of the opposite sex.

It didn't make sense. Any of it.

'It's straight on here.'

Miles changed gear to negotiate the roundabout. 'Why couldn't Russell drive Sam home?' he asked without looking across at her.

'Ben's asleep and he didn't want to wake him. Didn't I say that?'

'I don't know.' Miles frowned. He couldn't remember her telling him that, but he was sure she'd told him her ex-husband had a girlfriend. *Stefanie*, wasn't it? Or maybe he was leaping to conclusions and they didn't live together. It was none of his business, but he really wanted to know.

'Does he live alone?' he asked carefully.

He felt her head shake in denial. 'He's bought the flat with his girlfriend, but...' Jemima paused to consider what she was going to say '...she... isn't particularly maternal, apparently.'

'Then why get involved with a man who has two children?' he asked without thinking.

Jemima smiled and brushed at her hair. 'Makes you wonder, doesn't it? Russell really loves the boys too, so she's on to a loser if she thinks he'll forget about them. He won't. If it's a choice between her and the boys, he'll pick the boys.' She sat back in her seat. 'But I suppose Stefanie didn't know that about him when they got together.' Her eyes flicked across to him. 'They met at work. So she wouldn't necessarily have known what she was taking on, would she?'

Anyone with an ounce of sense would factor that in as a significant risk. Miles made a non-committal response. He could see why Stefanie might not want to drive a sick boy to her boyfriend's ex-wife, but where was the problem with taking care of a sleeping child?

'You take a left at the next junction.'

Miles made the turn. 'Is she at the flat tonight?'

'I don't know. I didn't ask.' Jemima looked at him. 'It wouldn't make any difference. Ben doesn't like her. Russell couldn't leave him with her in case he woke up while he was out. If that happened he'd have a difficult job to get him to stay again.'

Interesting. But still none of his business, Miles reminded himself. He couldn't help but admire the way Jemima had carefully avoided being vitriolic towards her ex-husband or his new girlfriend. That was rare, in his experience. Most people couldn't resist the opportunity to dish the dirt. Human nature, he supposed.

But Jemima hadn't done that. For the second time in a very short space of time it occurred to him how lucky Ben and Sam were in their mother. It clearly cost her to let her boys see their father regularly, but she did absolutely nothing to get in the way of it. Contrast that with his own mother, who'd made it her personal mission to make sure he didn't have a male role model anywhere in his life.

'It's here,' Jemima said, pointing a little way up the wide tree-lined road. 'Just after the next junction. On the left.'

Russell Chadwick might live in a flat, but it was an expensive one. Miles felt a simmering anger when he compared the elegant art deco façade with the run-down family home he'd conceded to his ex-wife. The man ought to be horse-whipped.

Jemima was out of the car seconds after he'd pulled to a stop. 'I won't be long.'

Miles watched as she hurried up the steps and bent to speak into a metal grid on the side wall. She pushed the door open and disappeared inside the entrance.

Miles stood with his back against the bonnet of his car. The street lights were amber orbs in a dark clear sky…and it was cold. He pulled up his jacket collar and tucked his hands into the pockets.

What was he doing here? Saturday night… No, it was Sunday morning. But the question remained the same. What in heaven's name had possessed him to be here doing this? He never…

The door opened and Jemima appeared carrying a small backpack. A man with a young boy in his arms was closely behind her. *Sam's father?* It had to be. Miles stood straight. As they walked down the steps he opened the car door and pulled the front seat forward, turning back to face them.

'This is Russell,' Jemima said as soon as she was close enough. 'Sam, climb in the back and I'll come and sit next to you.'

Russell lowered the pyjama-clad boy to the ground and he scrambled into the back seat. Even in the dark Miles could see that Sam's face was pale and entirely miserable. Miles watched as Jemima smiled encouragingly at her son and leant in to hand the ice cream tub across. The backpack she tucked in the front.

Miles turned his attention to Sam's father. Russell Chadwick looked ordinary. He was of average height, average build and of average colouring. Miles felt a curious sense of relief. God only knew why.

Jemima stood straight. 'Sorry, I should have introduced you properly. Russell, this is Miles Kingsley.'

Automatically Miles held out his hand, his eyes firmly meeting Russell Chadwick's. Unlike Jemima, who appeared to be thinking of nothing but her son, he was completely aware of what Russell was assuming about why he was here and what that must mean about Jemima's relationship with him. Moreover, he was fairly sure the other man didn't like it.

'Miles,' Russell said.

He nodded in acknowledgment.

Russell put his hands in his trouser pockets. 'It was good of you to come and pick Sam up.'

This was probably a clear case of too much tes-
tosterone, but Miles didn't like Russell Chadwick
one bit. He smiled. 'Jemima only had to ask. She's
very special.'

He watched the dawning recognition in the other
man's eyes that they had locked antlers as sure as
if they were two stags. Miles couldn't remember
when he'd disliked a man more.

'Sam's not at all well.'

'So I gathered. I was with Jemima when you
phoned.' Miles resisted the temptation to add, *We
were about to go to bed.* It wouldn't have been
true…and he wasn't sure whether Jemima would
play along with it.

Russell shuffled his feet. 'I'd tried to get her
earlier.'

It was a gift. Irresistible. 'Yes, we'd not long
walked through the door,' Miles replied and put a
deliberate arm round Jemima's waist.

He'd intended it to be punishment for the man
who'd hurt Jemima so much, a physical act of
support, but as soon as his fingers splayed out on
the soft curve of her hip he forgot that original
purpose.

Russell Chadwick could have fallen down dead
on the pavement and Miles wouldn't have noticed.
Nothing about her ex-husband mattered. His
fingers were alive to the fact that he was touching
Jemima. Beneath his hand she was soft and warm.

This close to her, he could smell the soft scent of her perfume, so light it hovered at the edge of his consciousness. He could see the tiny pulse beating in her neck. He was used to being around women, but the effect of the long white column of her neck and the dark burnished copper of her hair sent his libido into the stratosphere.

And then she looked up—her pale face surrounded by that cloud of red curls, her mouth softly parted and her eyes a shimmering green...

It felt natural. Inevitable. He was going to kiss her. He knew it and the flare in her green eyes told him she knew it too. Miles moved slowly and caught the soft 'oh' she uttered in his mouth. His hands spread out on the linen of her dress, feeling the curves that lay beneath it.

His head was pounding with her name. He could never have expected how amazing this would feel. Her lips were warm and pliant beneath his. It was just a kiss... Not important, he thought as he let his tongue flick out. She was... *Oh, God.*

Who was he trying to kid? There were kisses and there were kisses. Miles pulled her in closer as he deepened the kiss. The temptation was to let his hands slide down over the gentle curves of her buttocks. Pull her in really close.

She was lovely. Really, really lovely.

He heard the soft murmur in the back of her throat, whether passion or protest he didn't know.

And then Jemima moved to rest her hands against his chest. Every sinew in his body resisted, but he obediently pulled back to look into her eyes. She was so near he could feel her breath on his lips. *What was she thinking?*

'Sam,' she said huskily, her green eyes darker than he'd ever seen them.

It was a moment before he realised she was talking about her son, sitting feet away in the car. Regretfully Miles moved away. He felt cold without her. Shaken. 'We'd better get him home.'

'Y-yes.' Jemima gave him a half smile and moved towards the car. 'Bye, Russell. I'll see you tomorrow,' she said carelessly over her right shoulder.

It was beautifully done. It would have left Russell with exactly the impression Miles had intended, but…*what had he been thinking of?*

This wasn't a game. Despite every promise he'd ever made to himself about never getting mixed up with a single mother, he'd kissed her. And it was addictive. He knew exactly how it felt to have her soft curves pushed up against him and he knew he wanted more…

But that wasn't going to happen. He wasn't the kind of man who was capable of stepping in to play happy families. He had no experience of one. Nothing to contribute. Miles walked round to the driver's side, climbed in and shut the door.

He'd wanted to help her and yet he'd just made everything extremely complicated. If Rachel got wind of the fact he was messing about with the emotions of her friend she'd be justifiably angry. Alistair had warned him Jemima was brittle. She'd described herself as 'walking wounded' and the last thing he wanted to do was hurt her any more than she'd already been hurt.

Damn it! He should have remembered that... He shouldn't have tried to play stupid mind games with a man he probably wouldn't see again... He shouldn't...

'Miles?'

He looked over his shoulder. Half of Jemima's face was in shadow, but he knew she was smiling.

'Thank you,' she said softly.

Two tiny words and yet they had the power to remove any sense of regret. In the mirror he met her steady green gaze. She'd understood exactly why he'd kissed her...and she was grateful.

'You're welcome.'

Jemima glanced over her shoulder and gave a tiny wave to Russell, who was still standing on the pavement. 'I don't think he quite believes it.'

'Oh, I don't know,' Miles said, glancing in his wing mirror. Russell Chadwick looked like a man in shock to him. Perhaps he'd just been reminded of how fantastic the woman he'd walked out on was. He certainly hoped so.

Miles set the car in first gear as she gave a soft laugh, halfway between a gurgle and a hiccup. *Jemima was entirely surprising…*and she was *very* welcome. In fact, he'd be happy to kiss her any time she liked—with or without the audience. Except, of course, he wouldn't. Kissing Jemima Chadwick was a very foolish thing to do.

'Do you need me to direct you back?' Jemima asked, leaning forward.

Miles shook his head. 'I can remember the way.'

He heard her settle back in her seat. Another swift glance in his rear-view mirror saw Jemima place her arm around her son with the other hand clutching the empty ice cream tub.

'How is he doing?' Miles smiled to himself in the darkness. *Perhaps he didn't want to know the answer to that*.

'Who are you?' A young voice spoke from the depths of the blanket. 'Mum, why aren't we in our car?'

Jemima answered him in a matter of fact voice. 'Because it's broken down again. I had to leave it outside Rachel's house.'

'But who is he?'

Miles let his eyes flick to the rear-view mirror again. For one moment his gaze locked with Jemima's, no doubt they were both wondering whether Sam had seen the kiss. That had been such an irresponsible thing for him to do. The thought that a vulnerable five-year-old might be watching hadn't occurred to him.

Jemima broke eye-contact first. 'This is Miles, Sam. He's Alistair's best friend and he offered to help me come to get you when Daddy rang to say you were not feeling very well.'

'Oh.' And then, after a pause, 'He's got a very small car.'

Miles couldn't help but listen while Jemima explained about classic cars and how some people enjoyed driving really old cars and liked to get together with other people who drove the same sort of old car. It was a kind of club, she said.

He glanced back via the mirror. Hearing his passion put into words like that made it seem rather ridiculous—and he got the feeling she was doing it deliberately. Jemima might have been bruised by her life experiences, but inside she had a wicked sense of humour which was bubbling just beneath the surface.

And he liked the sound of her voice. It was the kind of pitch that sat easily on the ears. She could probably read a telephone directory and make it sound like Wordsworth. It had an innate musicality to it.

In fact, he realised with a shock, he liked *her*. Genuinely…liked her.

Miles pulled up outside her house, reversing neatly into a tight space. He heard Jemima murmur, 'We're home, sweetheart,' as he climbed out and walked round to the passenger side, pulling the front seat forward.

Jemima unwound herself from the tight seating position and stood on the pavement. She pushed back her bright curls as the wind caught them. 'Well, we made it without mishap,' she said, holding up the ice cream tub.

He felt a smile curve his mouth. 'I'm not disappointed about that.'

'I bet.' Then her smile faltered. 'Miles, thank you.' She stopped awkwardly. 'It's really late and I'm—'

Miles stopped her with a shake of the head and a light brush of his fingers against her cheek. He probably shouldn't have done that either. It was those eyes. Truly like windows into the soul—and her soul was beautiful. *She* was beautiful. How had he missed that during the past two weeks?

And she wasn't interested in him. He could see that from the wary look that flashed into her green eyes. In front of her ex-husband she might let him kiss her, but now… It was a clear no.

Salutary.

He didn't think it had ever happened before.

Miles moved backwards. 'Is Sam in his slippers? Do you want me to carry him in?'

'I can manage.' She leant into the car. 'Out you come, Sam. Let's get you into bed.' Her voice was brusque and capable, much more like the Jemima Chadwick he knew from the office.

Sam emerged wrapped in a blanket, his dark hair tousled and his eyes big and shining. Clutched in his hand was the duvet and it was immediately obvious that Jemima wasn't going to be able to carry everything.

'Leave the duvet, sweetheart. Let's get you inside and I'll come back for it in a minute.'

Miles looked directly at Sam. 'Do you mind if I carry you into the house for your mum? Then she can bring in all your things.'

The eyes, just peeking out from the top of the blanket, seemed to consider it for a moment and then a small voice said, 'I don't mind.'

Miles bent down and picked him up. He was surprisingly heavy.

Jemima looked at them briefly and then bent to pull out the overnight bag and duvet. 'Thanks,' she said, shutting the car door. 'How do I lock it?'

'Don't worry about it. It's late, there's no one around and I'll be gone in a minute.'

Jemima rummaged in her handbag for her front door keys. 'Sorry, I should have got these out earlier. I'm keeping you waiting…'

Miles shifted Sam in his arms. 'How are you feeling?' he asked him, thinking he should say something.

'Better.'

'That's good.'

The eyes looked at him steadily. 'I hate being sick.'

'Everyone does.' Miles watched as Jemima hurriedly opened the front door. 'There you go,' he said to Sam as he lowered him inside. Then he looked up at Jemima and felt…tongue-tied.

What did you say to your temporary secretary whose young son was watching and who you wanted to kiss again very much? There was only one thing that could be said. He stepped backwards. 'I'll leave you to it. He looks like he ought to be in bed.'

'I know.' Her hand came out to rest on her son's head, her long fingers moving through the dark curls. 'I don't know how I would have managed without you…'

'It was nothing.' Miles raised a hand in a gesture of goodbye and walked back towards the car. The front door shut before he was even halfway there. He took a moment to look back. His smile was self-deprecating. It had been a strange evening. Very strange.

And Jemima Chadwick….

Without question she was a very interesting woman—and, for entirely different reasons than before, he still wasn't sure what to make of her.

CHAPTER SIX

MONDAY morning seemed to whip round more quickly than Jemima could have believed possible. There hadn't been time to draw breath, let alone decide how it would be best to play the day ahead of her.

Before she knew it she was squeezed into an overcrowded tube carriage and heading into Covent Garden. Commuting wasn't an activity she found particularly conducive to thought, but she was tending towards the idea that the only sensible thing to do was to carry on exactly as before. She could take her cue from Miles as to whether he wanted to acknowledge at work that they had mutual friends.

And the kiss?

Was probably best forgotten.

Sam didn't seem to have seen it. At least he hadn't mentioned any kiss and she thought he would have done if he'd observed anything. So that was good, but it hadn't stopped her thinking about it. Throughout most of yesterday, if she were honest. Jemima smiled to herself. It had been... lovely.

She'd always thought kissing was a little over-rated, but that was because she hadn't been kissed by an expert before. When she stopped to think about it, it made sense really that there would be virtuosos in kissing as in everything else. Clearly Miles Kingsley was one of those. Her insides seemed to curl up at the edges when she thought about how it had felt.

Miles had made her feel...priceless. For those few moments she'd felt spectacularly desirable. Of course she knew it was an illusion. One glance in her bedroom mirror had told her that. In reality she was a slightly overweight mother of two who needed to do some abdominal exercises before she could do justice to any of the clothes in her wardrobe, borrowed or otherwise.

Besides, it hadn't meant anything. It wasn't as though Miles had been overcome with passion. He'd only kissed her to support her in front of Russell. *She could almost fall in love with him for that alone.* Jemima smiled again. It might not be particularly mature, but it had felt fantastic seeing Russell's reaction as they'd driven away. Just the possibility that he might have believed a man like Miles could seriously be in love with her was so funny. Absolutely, delightfully...funny.

Jemima walked round from Leicester Square towards the Kingsley and Bressington building, her stomach beginning to churn in anticipation of… She wasn't quite sure what. It couldn't be the prospect of seeing Miles because she wasn't that stupid. There was nothing about a man like Miles Kingsley that made him right for her even if… Well, if…

She preferred to think her newfound sense of optimism came from a belief in the infinite possibilities of life. Despite the leaky bathroom and the prospect of losing the boys for two whole weeks when Russell took them to Spain on holiday she felt…hopeful.

Of course, it would have been better if she could have conjured up a stunning designer outfit for work this morning. Something spectacular that would have assuaged the wound to her feminine pride caused by the 'dresses like her mother' jibe.

But that wasn't a possibility. She was back in Joshua's mum's perfectly sensible, if a little dull, redundant work clothes. She couldn't justify it with her conscience to siphon off part of her first pay cheque when Ben needed new school shoes, even though it was so near the end of term and his feet were bound to grow another size before September.

Besides, the whole purpose of taking a temp job this side of the school holidays was that she'd have some money to take the boys out over the summer break and she'd already promised them a trip to Legoland.

But it would have been nice to have bought a new dress. Just one. Jemima allowed herself a small sigh and pushed open the door to Kingsley and Bressington, taking consolation from the fact that she'd allowed herself a little more time than usual to straighten her hair and had made a fairly good job of smearing on a touch of make-up. Nothing so revolutionary that Miles would notice—or comment on. She couldn't bear it if he thought she was taking the kiss thing too seriously and making an effort for him. She'd die of embarrassment.

The door to his office when she got there was, thankfully, shut. Jemima opened the tall cupboard and carefully tucked her handbag towards the back, glad she had a moment or two to settle herself.

'How is he?'

Jemima jumped at the sound of his voice. She whirled round with a gasp.

Miles smiled, leaning nonchalantly against the door frame. 'Sorry, I didn't mean to startle you.'

'I hadn't realised you were here yet,' she said, feeling foolish. He was in another sharp suit. He must own hundreds. This one was more black than grey and the tie was the colour of a ripe Victoria plum. The overall effect was, frankly, very sexy.

'I was in at seven. How's Sam doing?'

'He's fine.' Her voice sounded breathless, even to her own ears. Her throat had constricted so much it was difficult to get any words out at all. She'd thought Miles in casual wear was more lethal than Miles in a city suit, but she discovered she was wrong.

He seemed even sexier than before—*now she knew what it felt like to be kissed by him,* that voice in her head whispered. More intimidating too— *now she'd been kissed by him.*

Oh…*hell.*

She had to stop thinking like this. Jemima made a determined effort not to let her eyes wander to his lips and tried again. 'I think Sam must have eaten too many sweets because he was fine all day Sunday. Nothing the matter with him at all.'

Much better, she thought, turning away to lock the cupboard door. Cool, calm and composed. That was what she was aiming for.

'I wasn't really expecting you in today.'

Jemima's stomach fell something like three feet and her body temperature plummeted. *Why?* Why wouldn't she be in to work today? Why would Miles think that? Had she embarrassed him by too enthusiastically responding to his kiss? Her mind conjured up an image of the way she'd melted against him…

Oh, God. Please, no. She hadn't mumbled incoherently, had she? Had she seemed too grateful for the attention?

She was going to die of mortification if he thought she thought he'd meant it all seriously. She hadn't for one moment considered that he'd be expecting her not to turn up. She'd promised Amanda she'd stick out the full assignment whatever happened and…

Miles cut across her panicked thoughts. 'Sam looked so woebegone. I thought he'd certainly be off school today and want you with him. If you need to be there for him, just put seven and a half hours down for today regardless and go home.'

Jemima couldn't quite believe Miles had just offered to pay her for a day she didn't work. She'd *never* let him do that. It was kind, but…

Why would he do that for her? He hardly knew her—and the fact that her best friend was marrying his best friend hardly constituted a friendship.

'He's fine. Really.'

'You're sure?'

'Yes.' *He must feel really sorry for her.* Jemima hated the way everyone seemed to feel so sorry for her. She was so…tired of being an object of pity. It irked her that she had been forced to accept so much help. It was kind of everyone, but…

Couldn't they see that only part of the reason behind her trying to build some kind of career for herself was financial? The other part was a desire for independence. She wanted to prove to herself, to her family…to Russell…that she could manage perfectly well on her own.

Miles must have been able to read something of what she was thinking because he added quickly, 'If it would help I could send you home with a couple of audio tapes and you could email everything through later on.'

Jemima shook her head. 'That's really nice of you, but Sam's absolutely okay and back at school.' She nodded as though to emphasise the truth of what she'd said, then walked over and sat behind her desk. There was no need to add that it wasn't an option anyway since her computer, like her car, had given up the ghost.

'I'm glad he's feeling so much better,' Miles said, straightening up and pulling a hand through his hair. She then watched, fascinated, as a smile twisted his sensual mouth. 'I suppose,' he said slowly, 'I'm still haunted by the prospect of him actually using the ice cream tub—'

She went to speak, but Miles stopped her.

'—even if it did have a lid.'

Jemima felt a bubble of laughter form in the pit of her stomach. 'I wasn't going to say that.'

'Really?'

His eyebrows lifted the merest fraction, but it brought her laughter to the surface. 'Okay. No, you're right. I was going to say that,' she conceded.

She pulled back a wayward strand of hair and re-clipped it tightly in her simple hairgrip. 'But the lid is important. It keeps—'

'I get the picture.'

Jemima laughed again and leant forward to boot up her computer.

He seemed to hesitate for a moment and then he asked, 'Have you had a chance to speak to your plumber this morning?'

She shook her head, before keying in the password. 'I did try his mobile before I got on the tube but it was switched off. I left a message and I'll give it another go when I go for a coffee break later.'

'If there's any problem with getting him to come back, I've got the number of my plumber with me. He's good. I've worked with him on the last three projects. His name is Steve Baldock.'

Jemima looked up. 'Thanks.'

'It's in my briefcase. Let me know if you want it.'

'I will, thanks.'

'It makes sense to ring the man you used first. If he's to blame he'll have to put it right without charging you.'

'Yes, I know.'

Miles hesitated, as though he would like to have continued talking. He looked as uncomfortable as she felt. *Strange*. Then he pulled a hand through his dark hair again. 'I suppose I'd better get on,' he said abruptly.

Perhaps he felt uncomfortable about the change in their relationship. He needn't worry. She wasn't about to take advantage of the fact that they had mutual friends.

'I'll grab a coffee, if that's okay? Then I'll get started on all this,' she said, indicating the large pile of files and papers he'd placed in her in-tray some time between when she'd left on Friday and now. 'I missed breakfast this morning. Hopefully the caffeine will stave off my craving for chocolate until lunch time.'

'Was it a rush to get out?'

Jemima stood up. 'It's always a rush in my house. This morning it was a particular disaster because Ben suddenly remembered he'd forgotten to learn his spellings for a test they're having today. He should've done them over the weekend but, of course, he was with Russell.'

'Couldn't he take them with him?'

'He could, but how many eight-year-olds do you know can manage to organise their work like that? Ben forgets about things like homework the minute he walks out the school gate.' She paused at the door. 'I'm going to have to remember to make a point of asking him when I get in. Do you want a coffee?'

'That would be great. Thanks.' Miles stepped

back and closed the door to his office. What was happening to him? He couldn't quite believe he'd offered to pay her for a day she didn't work. He thrust a hand through his hair. He hadn't meant to say that; the words had seemed to say themselves.

Jemima had changed, but more worryingly *he* had changed. The truth was he didn't know anything about how eight-year-olds organised their homework. He'd never before experienced the slightest interest in the subject, but he found he was very interested in Jemima. By extension that seemed to mean he was interested in her sons. And he certainly felt an overwhelming compulsion to try and help her.

Why was that? He liked to think he was a fairly compassionate person, but Jemima's problems were just that—hers. He shouldn't be trying to think of ways to make her life simpler. She was a grown woman, more than capable of finding an alternative plumber by herself if she needed one.

Miles frowned and walked across to the window. There was nothing much to see, just a narrow London street typical of the area. He let out his breath in a controlled stream.

He hadn't known what to expect from this morning. From Jemima or himself. How he would feel about working with her, seeing her…

He'd told her that he hadn't expected her to be at work today, but actually that had been a lie. He *had* expected her to be there. In fact, he'd been watching the clock and listening out for her arrival—not consciously, but he'd known the minute she'd walked into the office. He'd heard the door open and had been on his feet.

Jemima, he'd decided, was big on duty. If she said she'd do something then it would have to be something truly catastrophic to make her break her word. She'd come in to work—and he'd wanted to make it easy for her to go home again.

But…offering to pay a temporary secretary for a day not worked was surely taking it all a bit too far.

Of course, he hadn't liked the idea of Sam being sent to a childminder and desperately wanting his mum—and he knew why that was. It was an uncomfortable echo of his own childhood and Sam's small pale face peeking out from a blanket was a haunting image.

But it was none of his business. Jemima Chadwick was a friend of a friend, his very temporary secretary, and her life was absolutely none of his business.

Damn it! Miles turned abruptly from the window and went to sit down at his desk. He picked up his pen and idly started to twist it between his long fingers. Jemima was also a single mother with responsibilities. And that was the one reason above all others why he shouldn't be contemplating any kind of relationship with her.

Miles started drawing straight lines on his pad of paper and then put in the horizontal ones. He needed to focus on how hurt children could get when the adults in their life brought home new partners. *He'd* been hurt when his own mother had done it.

Miles shaded in a couple of the small boxes. He wasn't even particularly comfortable with finding a mother sexually attractive. There was something wrong with that somehow. As though the two things were, or at least should be, mutually exclusive.

But, astoundingly, he was attracted to Jemima. No question about that. She'd returned to her work uniform—but it wasn't as good a camouflage as before. Her hair might be pulled straight and drawn back in a way that concealed how stunning it could look, but he wasn't fooled. Beneath the conventional and dull clothes was someone altogether more interesting.

And he knew what it felt like to kiss her...

The door opened and he had to watch Jemima as she carried in his coffee. He remembered her green eyes wide with surprise and the small gasp she'd made as he'd finally closed the distance between them. Then there was the way her body had felt so soft and inviting, the way she'd responded.

Jemima placed his coffee carefully on the

leather coaster—and it was difficult to make his throat work. 'Thanks.' His voice sounded husky.

He couldn't quite place what it was that had made that kiss feel so special. He'd kissed many, many women over the past two decades, but he wasn't sure he'd ever experienced anything quite like it. There'd been a…sweetness about it—and he wanted to kiss her again.

'You're welcome. It's an addiction, though.'

Jemima smiled at him and he felt his mouth curve into an inane grin. 'I know.' It wasn't just the coffee that was addictive. 'And I'm told it stains my teeth.'

Her mouth quirked with suppressed laughter. 'Who dared tell you that?'

'Some people have no ability socially, so one has to make allowances,' he said, loving the sparkle that appeared in her usually serious eyes.

Miles twisted the pen in his hand. There was nothing contrived or artificial about Jemima. How had he missed that? He should have been able to see past the unflattering clothes to notice how beautiful she really was from the very beginning.

'It's quite true that coffee stains your teeth, though,' Jemima said, turning back towards the door. 'I read it somewhere. Did you also know that champagne gives you halitosis?'

'Is that true?'

'No idea. Bit depressing if it is.'

Miles let the laughter warm his eyes. 'Very.'

'Though I don't know why I say that. I don't actually like champagne.'

Didn't she? 'What do you drink?'

'From choice?'

He nodded.

'Pimms, I think. During the summer, anyway.' Jemima's hand was on the door handle. 'Or a nice dry white wine. I'm not particularly fussed about the country of origin or the price of the bottle because I think it's a con.'

'Do you?' he asked with a faint lift of his expressive eyebrows, knowing that she would understand why. He wasn't disappointed. He watched with enjoyment as Jemima bit her lip.

'You're a wine connoisseur, aren't you?'

Miles burst out laughing. ''Fraid so.'

'Oops.' She shot him a mischievous smile. 'I wouldn't have said that if I'd known. That would have been rude.'

'I don't believe you,' Miles said softly, watching for her reaction.

Jemima gave a rich chuckle as she went out and shut the door. It was strange how he'd thought she was so serious when he'd first met her. Despite all the troubles and disappointments of her life, the one thing that had emerged intact was her sense of humour.

Quiet, disciplined, conscientious—all those

things were still true, but there was a hidden side of her personality. It was a side he longed to know more about.

But at what cost? Particularly to her. He needed to remember that Jemima had troubles enough without the complication of a man like him wafting in and out of her life. And 'temporary' was all he wanted…or was capable of.

Jemima spread some butter on her toast. The trouble with mornings, in her opinion, was that they happened too early. She needed at least a couple of coffees in her system before she was ready to face the day. She smiled. Better not let Miles suspect that about her.

'Ben. Sam,' she called. 'Hurry up and come downstairs for breakfast. I've made porridge.' She listened to the absolute silence above. 'Grandma will be here in a minute.'

She glanced down at her wrist-watch. At least she hoped Grandma would be here in a minute or she was going to be cutting it fine to get to work by nine-thirty. Her third week at Kingsley and Bressington had flown by. Halfway through her stint there she could almost say she was enjoying it.

Having had no interest in public relations before she'd started at Kingsley and Bressington she'd developed a healthy respect for it. Certainly a respect for Miles. He was absolutely brilliant at what he did and the hours he put in were punishing.

Unbelievably, she was going to miss it all when it was over. *Miss Miles* too, if she were honest, though she'd seen less of him this week than in the previous two. For much of the time he'd been shut away in his office, emerging only for long working lunches. Yesterday almost the only sign he was in the building was the enormous pile of work he'd left in her in-tray.

Nevertheless there was a buzz about working at Kingsley and Bressington and there was always the prospect of seeing Miles. A five minute conversation with him and her day seemed that little bit brighter. It was probably just as well her time working for him was limited.

'Ben. Can you hear me?' She bit into her toast as the telephone started to ring.

Chewing quickly, she grabbed the phone. 'Hello.'

'Jemima, I'm so glad I caught you,' Rachel began, her voice sounding strained, though that might have been because the reception was so poor.

'Wherever are you?' Jemima asked, frowning. 'You sound like you're in a dishwasher.'

'I'm at the airport.'

'Airport?' She hadn't expected that reply. Rachel never travelled abroad for work, so what was she doing there? Jemima looked up as Ben walked sleepily into the kitchen. She motioned for him to sit at the breakfast bar.

'It's Alistair's dad. He's had some kind of hae-morrhage. His stepmother called and said we need to fly out to be there…in case.'

Jemima felt as if she'd stumbled into one of those television adverts where you could freeze time but still be functioning yourself. Everything around her seemed to stop. There was just her moving about as she walked over to put her toast down on a plate. 'Is it serious?'

'Apparently.' The line crackled, making it diffi-cult to hear. 'Jemima, are you still there?'

'Yes, I'm here.'

'He's lost a lot of blood, but I think the concern is that they don't know why it happened. It's going to be a while before we know.'

'How's Alistair?' Jemima asked quickly.

'He just wants to get out to Canada as soon as we possibly can. He's telephoned his mum and let her know…'

Jemima pulled her mind into focus. She needed to think clearly and logically. 'Okay. Right. What do you need me to do?' she asked, sitting down on the bar stool next to Ben.

By the time Rachel had finished speaking she had a list which ranged from asking the next door neighbour if she would push the post through the door to hiring a marquee for the wedding.

'Are you okay with all that?' Rachel asked.

Jemima wrote the word 'medieval' next to the

word 'marquee' as a reminder—though she was unlikely to forget. How did you go about finding a medieval-style marquee for a wedding in rural Kent at such short notice?

'Fine,' she said, trying to imbue her voice with confidence. 'I'll work my way down your list. If you think of anything else…' Jemima gave up trying to say anything for a moment because it was obvious Rachel hadn't got a hope in hell of catching what she was saying.

She drew a deep breath and read down Rachel's list.

'Alistair has rung Miles to let him know what's happened,' Rachel said as soon as the line cleared a fraction.

'Miles?'

'Miles Kingsley. His best man. You met him at dinner.'

'Oh, yes,' Jemima said, cursing herself for being all kinds of a fool.

'Do you want his number?'

Dutifully Jemima jotted down the telephone number of Kingsley and Bressington. It would have been so much easier now, would have felt so much more honest, if she'd owned up that she was working there temporarily.

Rachel continued, 'He said he'd help. That's his work number, but I think he practically lives there.'

'Okay, I'll get in contact with him.'

She heard her mother's key in the front door. 'Jemima?'

'Hang on a second,' she said to Rachel. 'In the kitchen, Mum. I'm on the phone.'

The line broke up again, so much that it was impossible to hear what was being said.

'Will you let me know how Alistair's dad is doing?' Jemima said in the hope that Rachel was hearing her better. She ripped off the front sheet of her lined A4 pad and tucked it into the side pocket of her handbag.

'Give Alistair my love.' The reception was truly appalling. Jemima struggled to make sense of the crackling noise at the other end before she gave up and ended the call.

Her mum walked into the kitchen. 'Trouble?'

'Rachel's father-in-law-to-be is ill. I don't know any of the details because the line was breaking up all the time, but they're flying out to Toronto today.'

'Oh, no. So close to the wedding. What a dreadful thing to have happened.'

Jemima glanced down at her watch and picked up her sandwiches from the worktop. 'Is it okay if I'm a little late back? I need to do a couple of things for Rachel at the flat.'

'Of course, darling,' her mother said. 'You'd better hurry or you'll be late for work. I meant to be here ten minutes ago, but the parking around here is so atrocious.'

'I know.' Jemima went through a mental check of everything she needed to have done and needed to take with her. 'There's some talk of it all being permit parking only, which will help.'

She kissed one finger and placed it on Ben's hair, a concession to his belief that all kisses were too wet. 'Have a good day. Sam,' she called from the bottom of the stairs. 'I've got to go.'

Sam came scampering down the staircase and gave her a quick hug. 'Is Grandma in the kitchen?'

Jemima nodded and watched as he ran through to find her. 'Bye,' she called out as she shut the door behind her. There was no reply. The boys were too busy talking about Ben's forthcoming birthday party. He would be nine—she couldn't quite believe time had gone so fast.

And that was another thing she was going to have to find time to do. Ben needed a birthday present and there was no way she could afford the Xbox she knew he really wanted.

It wasn't as though she particularly wanted him to spend all his free time playing on one, but 'all his friends had one' and she felt guilty. That sharp knife twisted a little more as she felt there was something else she wasn't able to provide for her sons.

Of course, Russell could—and he probably would. That hurt almost as much. Jemima hurried along the pavement towards the tube station. Thank goodness she had this job. She had to keep every-thing in perspective and keep positive. Things were going to get better.

If she dropped her time sheet off with Amanda tonight she could pick up her cheque personally rather than wait for the post. If she did that the money would be cleared in her account in time for her to use it to buy something for Ben. Maybe, at a stretch, it might even be possible to be the parent who gave the present that would make her son's eyes light up. There'd be no harm in seeing how much an Xbox actually did cost.

It was all going to be fine. Everything was falling into place. Except, of course, she'd also got to make a detour to Rachel and Alistair's flat, not to mention find the time to hire a marquee, book a caterer, a florist and some kind of medieval-type musicians. And all for a wedding that was sched-uled to take place in under three months.

Let alone that she wanted to make it perfect. *But poor Alistair.* There was never a good time to lose a parent, but so close to their wedding it didn't bear thinking about.

Somewhere in the depths of her handbag her mobile phone started to ring. She stopped and made a frantic search for it in the dark depths of her bag.

'I gather we've got a wedding to organise,' Miles said into her ear as soon as she answered.

Jemima shifted her handbag to her other shoulder. 'How did you get this number?'

'Alistair gave it to me. I'm to offer my help. As best man he considers it my duty, even though I'm a confirmed wedding phobic and of doubtful use.'

Despite everything, Jemima could feel herself start to smile. 'Did he say that?'

'More or less. Where are you now?' he asked.

Even though she knew, Jemima automatically looked up at the huge sign. 'Rayners Lane. I'm outside the tube station. Why?'

'I thought you might want to take a detour and pick up Rachel's wedding box. Apparently it'll make everything easy.'

'So she says. It's in the kitchen by the kettle.' Jemima walked inside the station. 'I'll go and get it this evening. I can't go now or I'll be late for work.'

'Don't worry, I know the boss. He's prepared to be very understanding.'

What was it about Miles that kept her on the edge of laughter? Moments ago she'd been worried about all the responsibility of taking over the planning of Rachel's dream wedding, but with a handful of sentences he'd managed to twist the situation into something that would be almost enjoyable.

'Does that mean I can start charging you from now? An extra hour on my time sheet...'

'No.' She could hear the smile in his voice. 'But it means I'll buy you lunch while we go through Rachel's exacting requirements.' Then the line went dead.

Lunch with Miles.

How exactly did she feel about that?

CHAPTER SEVEN

MILES felt a vague sense of injustice. No doubt Alistair's father hadn't intended to inconvenience him by falling so ill, but the fact remained that his carefully laid plans to keep his distance from Jemima had come to nothing. And what really bothered him about it was that he was pleased.

He ended his call to Jemima with a feeling of smiling anticipation, and all because she'd agreed to accept his help with booking a few tedious things for an equally tedious wedding. He hated weddings. He hated the ridiculous top hat and cravat he almost always had to wear at them. He hated the long and usually poor quality speeches that made the whole business so interminably lengthy. His own excepted—obviously.

Miles played with the paper-clips in the Perspex box in front of him, letting them rise and fall. He didn't even believe in marriage as an institution. Not really. Why did two intelligent people, who purported to love each other, need a piece of paper to hold them together?

It made no *sense*. His mother was right about that. It was an outdated dinosaur of an institution that belonged... Miles smiled to himself, pleased at the neat symmetry of his thoughts. It was an outdated institution that belonged in *medieval* times.

If he believed Alistair and Rachel had thought of that and were silently laughing he would feel a darn sight better at spending his time trying to book various people who spent their professional lives taking money off other people who thought they'd achieve nirvana if the flowers matched the lining of the best man's jacket.

Miles stood up abruptly and walked through to the small kitchen area. His hands went through the practised procedure of making coffee while his mind tried to analyse why he felt so...

So...

He pulled a distracted hand through his hair. He wasn't quite sure how he did feel. All he knew was that he was ridiculously pleased to be having lunch with Jemima. It felt like a *result*. It made no sense at all, but that was how it felt and the suspicion slid into his mind that all he'd been waiting for had been an excuse to break his decision to keep his distance from her.

And that didn't make any sense at all. There was

nothing about Jemima that should draw him to her. In fact, there was a great deal which should have prevented it.

So *why*? Miles returned to his desk and sipped his coffee. The truth was he didn't know *who* Jemima was—and that was fascinating.

The realisation hit him with a sudden force that there were few people, if any, whom he couldn't sum up within the first few minutes of meeting them. But Jemima had him guessing.

There was a…tension between the image she presented to the world and the Jemima he suspected lurked beneath the surface. It was as though she'd got used to hiding behind an image she felt safe with. One that ensured people didn't notice her. *Couldn't hurt her?* Every so often a different Jemima would peek out from behind the façade. The Jemima she would have been if life hadn't acted like a pumice stone.

That was the Jemima that fascinated him—if she existed. And she might not. He pulled a lever file closer and began to flip through the neatly typed pages. Miles pulled a highlighter pen out of the pot before him and selected a sentence in the second paragraph to shade orange.

It was quite possible his interest in her was entirely altruistic then. He'd had a glimpse of what her life was like and he wanted things to be better for her. Nothing wrong with that.

So what was worrying him? It was just lunch. A

working lunch. An hour discussing weddings. Miles smiled. Not that risky then.

The trouble was, when the time came it didn't feel as though his interest in her was altruistic. It felt personal. And it felt very risky from the moment she looked up from the computer screen and smiled at him.

His mouth automatically curved in response— for no other reason than it had felt good to be smiled at. He'd had a pig of a morning and yet one smile seemed to put everything back into kilter.

'Ready for lunch?'

'Two seconds,' she said, turning back and carefully saving everything. 'Do you think I'm going to need an umbrella?'

Miles avoided watching her fingers moving over the keyboard by turning away. 'We're only going a few hundred yards and if there's a sudden shower we can take cover.'

'Okay.' Jemima stood up and walked over to the tall cupboard, pulling out her handbag and a plastic carrier bag. 'Rachel has given us so much to look through.'

Miles said nothing. He was watching the way her simple knee-length skirt moulded beautifully across her bottom. Jemima had great legs too. He remembered them from when she'd stood on her kitchen worktop to make a hole in the ceiling. Long, long legs…

Jemima reached up to adjust her hairclip. He swallowed and struggled not to notice how the thin fabric of her white blouse pulled tight across her chest.

'Oh.'

'What?'

She opened up her hand to show two broken pieces of brown plastic. 'My hairclip's broken.'

Dark red hair fell round her face and Miles felt a tightening in his groin area. *Very, very risky*, a little voice whispered in his head. 'It looks good loose,' he said brusquely, turning towards the door.

'It doesn't. It looks a mess.' Jemima sighed. 'I've always wanted the kind of hair that was so smooth a hairgrip would slip out. Do you know what I mean?'

Hair like Verity Hunt's. Miles knew exactly what she meant. Hair that could be twisted into something that looked more like a sculpture. *Hair like her sister's*. Although he thought he understood why she wanted it, he also thought she was seriously undervaluing what nature had given her.

'It used to look better when I had layers cut into it. Still—' she shrugged and threw him a warm smile '—it doesn't really matter, does it.'

It suddenly seemed really important that she believed him. The way she looked probably shouldn't matter, but the way she felt about herself certainly did. 'If you want my opinion,' he said as he held the door open for her, 'I'd go for the curls. They're very sexy.'

He closed his eyes briefly. Had he actually said the word 'sexy' out loud? He hadn't meant to do that, but Jemima was certainly looking at him wide-eyed.

'Sexy?'

There was no backing away from it now. He pulled a smile into his eyes, searching for the ground between casual and complimentary. Something that wouldn't have him brought up before a sex-discrimination board. 'I think so.'

She just looked at him for a moment and then she laughed. 'I think men are strange.'

'No question,' he agreed easily. Miles led the way down the stairs. 'Although this should appeal to your practical nature…'

Jemima glanced across at him, a question in her equally sexy green eyes.

At the bottom of the stairs he leant in close to say quietly, 'Just think how much time you'd save in the morning if you didn't bother to straighten it.'

She gave a husky laugh. It ripped through his senses as much as the light rose-scented perfume that hung about her.

'Actually, that's quite a persuasive argument.'

'Felicity,' Miles said, pausing by the reception desk, 'Jemima and I are having a working lunch. I'm on my mobile if you need us.'

The receptionist's speculative glance did absolutely nothing to make him feel more relaxed. As they stepped outside Miles reached up and loosened his tie. It was becoming difficult to breathe, but then the air was muggy.

'So,' he said, making a real effort to keep his voice light and teasing, 'why do you hate your hair so much?'

'Because it's red.' She looked up and smiled—one of those inexpressibly sweet smiles that made him feel as if something intensely precious was being given to him.

'Mainly that, I think. There's no hiding when you have red hair. You always stand out. Wherever you go, whatever you do.'

'Isn't that a good thing?'

She laughed at him, changing the hand she was holding the carrier bag in. 'Only if you like that kind of attention. I leave all that to the other members of my family.'

From the little he knew of Verity Hunt, Miles imagined she did. Jemima seemed to echo what he was thinking. 'I'm the quiet one. Imogen is a natural campaigner, like my mum. They always seem to be working on some big issue or other.' She smiled across at him. 'Verity is an entertainer. She loves being the centre of everything.'

'And you?'

She laughed. 'Oh, I much prefer to keep in the

background. I don't like people talking about me and pointing me out. My dad used to say I was a "facilitator and nurturer" and that I'd get places because I'd slog away at it.'

Miles thought that was a good description of her. Quietly conscientious—but that didn't do justice to the wicked sense of humour she possessed. 'Used to?'

'He died. Three years ago.' Jemima changed the hand she was holding the carrier bag in for a second time. 'He was a fairly formidable man— but very lovely.'

It fascinated him hearing about her family. It began to make it easier to understand why she'd made some of the decisions she had. But if he'd hoped knowing more about her would assuage his curiosity, he was destined for disappointment.

He found the more she told him, the more he wanted to know. It was rather like playing pass the parcel. There was a prize beneath each layer of wrapping paper, but everyone knew the real treasure was found at the absolute centre of the parcel.

Miles reached out for the bag she was carrying and, after a moment's hesitation, she let him take it. 'This is heavy. What's Rachel got in here?' he asked, looking down.

'Her box file.' Jemima laughed, a sudden mischievous light shining in her green eyes. 'And just about every bridal magazine that's been published since Alistair proposed to her.'

'Really?'

'It's serious stuff.'

He peeked in the top of the bag. 'It would seem so.'

Jemima dodged a group of teenage backpackers. 'Rachel's even left me seven pages of detailed instructions. Apart from the fact that I hope Alistair's dad turns out not to be dangerously ill, I really hope she's not away too long. The sooner she takes back control of this extravaganza the better.'

Just that one glance in the top of the carrier bag had him silently echoing her sentiment. 'Considering we're not fans of the whole confetti and white ribbon scenario, we're not the best choice for this assignment, are we?' he remarked, turning the corner and walking down towards the piazza.

She didn't appear to be listening as her attention was caught by a living statue. Miles smiled, watching her expression as the 'Victorian lady' suddenly moved and startled a group of Japanese tourists. 'It's amazing how they do that. How does anyone keep still so long?'

'I couldn't do it.'

'I wouldn't want to. It must be so boring.' Jemima looked up at him. 'You know the boys would love it down here. I ought to bring them one weekend.'

'Why haven't you?'

'I don't know really.' She looked around at the milling crowds, the Italian-style piazza, the jugglers and mime artists. 'I suppose I just hadn't thought of it. I must, though. Perhaps it's something I could do for Ben's birthday.'

'When is it?'

'Saturday week.' For a moment her face crumpled, then he watched as she took control of whatever emotion was gripping her. 'He's going to be nine.'

'Is that what's bothering you? That he's growing up?'

She glanced across at him as he steered her towards the large glass-covered building. 'Of course not. Why did you think that?'

'My mother found it difficult. The passing of one's youth, I suppose…' He trailed off.

Miles watched her swallow. 'No. I don't feel like that. Each stage has been fun.' And then, 'Why do you think I'm upset?'

Miles merely smiled at her. He wasn't about to say that he'd spent the past week surreptitiously studying her. That he could read her expressions effortlessly and gauge her moods. He knew when she was typing something she found boring, when she couldn't read his handwriting, when she was thinking about something else…

And he knew when she was sad. Like now. It had washed over her quite suddenly.

Jemima shrugged. 'It's stupid really. Ben will be with his dad on his actual birthday.' She shot him a brave smile that twisted something inside him. 'It's the first time it's happened since Russell left. Not bad in almost three years, but I'm finding it difficult. It almost happened last year, but since our divorce was so recent Russell didn't push it. This year…' She bit her lip.

His reaction to her words surprised him. For a man with his background, a man whose mother must have been abroad for at least three of his childhood birthdays, he would have expected to feel very little empathy, but his pain surprised him. 'Is Ben having a party?'

'They're going bowling. Ben's really excited about it. He's not talked about much else all this week.'

Miles ran through the myriad responses open to him while the waiter took their order. The temptation was to accept what she said at face value. That was the socially acceptable thing to do. Or he could risk offering a sympathetic platitude or two. Or…he could say what he really thought.

'Hell, that's hard,' he said, as soon as the waiter walked out of hearing.

Sadness flickered across her face and she looked down.

'So are you going to do something special on a different day?' Miles asked, watching her closely. The last thing he wanted to do was to make her cry.

He reached out and played with the sugar sachets in the bowl in the centre of the table. 'You've got to remember I'm essentially very immature, but I'd be inclined to get in first and do something spectacular.'

Jemima looked up on a surprised laugh. 'It does make you want to do that.'

'What's stopping you? It's your weekend coming up isn't it?'

The instinctive response was 'money', but she knew it wasn't that. She wanted to behave well and responsibly. She didn't want Ben to guess how much she was hurting at the thought of not being at his party and not being able to tuck him up in bed on his birthday. He was coming up nine years old, for goodness' sake. She was the adult here. If she let on she was unhappy about it, she'd spoil it for him.

And it was ridiculous anyway, because she was going to see him first thing. She was going to be able to give him his present, see him open it...

'Do something tomorrow,' he said, watching her face.

Miles, Jemima decided, was one of life's problem solvers. Of course, she ought to do something fun tomorrow. She bit her lip and considered her options. First choice would be to take Ben and Sam on that long promised trip to Legoland, but her car was unlikely to make it that far. So...

She smiled. 'I could bring them here. Ben would love the transport museum and the street performers.'

'Would the boys like to see where you work?'

'I—I suppose they would—'

'Why don't you do that too? I'm going to be in work part of tomorrow. Bring them up and show them the office. Let them see where you go each day.'

Miles was a continual surprise to her. Jemima just looked across at him, a little stunned. Day after day she was falling just that little bit more under his spell. She'd never met anyone quite like him.

He was so supremely confident, fearsomely clever…handsome, naturally…and fun. Being with him was pure fun. Whenever she was with him she felt as though she were a different person. Much more like the woman she wanted to be.

'Okay.' She pulled at a strand of her hair. 'What shall I do? Ring you when we're here?'

'It's probably easiest.'

The waiter walked across with their drinks. Jemima had chosen a tall glass of freshly squeezed orange juice and she took a sip immediately. She would never, ever, have believed she'd be meeting Miles outside working hours, but then this wasn't exactly a date…

Just like this wasn't *exactly* a working lunch either.

'Have you got my mobile number?'

Jemima shook her head. 'Rachel gave me the Kingsley and Bressington one.' She felt a small bubble of laughter in the pit of her stomach. 'I felt daft pretending to write it down.'

He smiled, three tiny lines fanning out at the edges of his eyes.

She watched, fascinated, and then rushed in with, 'Did you ring Amanda and tell her what happened on Saturday?'

The glint in his blue eyes intensified. 'Oh, yes,' he said, drawing the words out.

'What did she say? Actually, what did *you* say? I don't want to contradict you. I'm going to see her this evening.'

Miles picked up his iced water. 'I told her about the dandelion. Since everyone appears to think it was a little naff, I thought Amanda might well agree.'

Jemima bit her lip, trying hard to stop the laughter which was threatening to engulf her. 'Did she?'

'Let's just say I don't think you're going to find the conversation very difficult at all.'

'Excellent.' Jemima gave up and laughed. After a moment, she wiped her eyes. 'Of course, tonight is the dandelion date.'

Actually that part of it wasn't so funny. It reminded her that, in some respects, Miles was still the man she'd first thought him. He was still the man who played the dating game as though it was, indeed, a game. As though the women he sent flowers to wouldn't care whether he sent flowers to a different woman the week after.

Perhaps they wouldn't. Perhaps it was only her who took everything so seriously. Maybe she was fifty years out of date. *Maybe even as boring as Russell had found her*.

'I hope you're taking Keira somewhere expensive. I think she deserves that after receiving a dandelion.' She kept her voice light. It was absolutely none of her business who Miles saw, but…

Jemima drew a deep breath and then smiled. 'I suppose we'd better get on with the purpose of our lunch.' She pulled the carrier bag on to her knee and lifted out the box file. 'It's a bit daunting,' she said, flicking through the contents of the bag. 'I think I'll leave the magazines in there and go through them this evening by myself. There might be some useful telephone numbers and websites in them.'

Miles opened the box file. 'What have we got here?' he said, spreading out a picture of a pink lined marquee on the table.

Jemima put the carrier bag back down on the floor and looked over. 'That's what Rachel doesn't want. It's too girly. We're looking for "medieval", remember. Though, to be honest, I think we'd be better trying to get a basic marquee and adding our own twelfth century touches,' she said seriously.

His eyes lit with laughter. 'Such as?'

She was ready for that one. 'I went to the library and got a book out on the period,' she said, reaching down and pulling it out from between the February and March editions of *Brides Today*. 'We probably could do something with heraldry.'

Miles turned it over and flicked the pages. 'How efficient,' he slid in lazily.

Jemima pulled out a notepad and headed it up with the words 'To Do'. 'That's why I'm such an excellent secretary.'

Miles laughed as she intended he should, but then he sat back in his chair, watching her. It made her feel uncomfortable, so it was almost a relief when he spoke. 'What *are* you going to do?'

She looked up, her pencil poised. 'About what?'

'Your career. You aren't going to be satisfied working as a temporary secretary for long. What's your long-term plan? I don't believe you haven't got one.'

Jemima smiled and returned to what she was doing. His words were a direct echo of her sisters'. Verity, because she didn't have children, had no concept of mother love and couldn't see there was any conflict of interest. Imogen, because she had a supportive husband who loved her and who had the kind of bank balance which made 'having it all' a distinct possibility.

Not her mum, though. Despite having had a highly successful career herself, her mum was a realist. She recognised that her situation had been very different from the one her middle daughter found herself in—and she was there for her, doing what she could to make things better. Jemima so loved her for it.

'Whatever I do is going to be a compromise,' she said, echoing something her mum had said to her when they'd been discussing the options.

'Between?'

She looked up again to find him still watching her intently. 'Ben and Sam come first. They have to.' He said nothing and she felt obliged to continue. 'That's part of the deal when you have children. I suppose, in the end, I'll settle for something near home.'

'Doing?'

Jemima smiled a little stiffly. She wasn't at all sure she wanted to be telling him all this. 'It doesn't really matter. I want to earn enough to finish the house and pay for some treats for the boys. I'm tired of telling them how sorry I am, but I don't have the money. It's not the earth I'm after.'

Miles looked thoughtful. He handed her back the book on medieval life as the waiter returned with their plates of pasta. 'In a decade or so Ben will be at university. You can't put everything on hold for ten years.'

'I know.' It was what she said to herself. It was *why* she'd gone to see Amanda. And *why* she'd taken a secretarial course.

It had seemed a reasonable compromise, but deep down she knew Miles was right. She did want more. Or, at least, the prospect of more. Being the least successful member of a high achieving family was difficult. But missing the boys' school sports day and never being home in time for tea wasn't an option either.

'So?' he prompted. 'What's your long-term plan?'

It was such a difficult question to answer. Jemima was acutely aware that in accepting the house in lieu of any claim on Russell's pension she had left herself vulnerable for the future.

And while Russell was never awkward about paying his contribution, how long would his girlfriend be happy with him paying out so much to his ex-wife?

And if Stefanie insisted he referred his payments back to the CSA she might find it wasn't worth her working at all, certainly not for the minimum wage. She could end up losing as much as she gained in a vicious catch-22.

Jemima picked up her fork. 'I haven't decided yet.' She looked across at him and forced a smile. 'I think I've become Amanda's project. It bothers her intensely that I've left myself unable to support myself and my children entirely alone. It offends her principles as a card carrying feminist…'

She stopped, suddenly reminded that Amanda's

views were very likely to be shared by Miles's mother. Hermione Kingsley was a fierce advocate of financial and emotional independence—whatever the latter actually meant when it was applied to the real world.

Did 'emotional independence' mean you couldn't let yourself love anyone because it was weakness to need any one other person? She'd never be able to truly believe that. Jemima concentrated on eating her pasta.

'Don't let Amanda bully you.'

She looked up, surprised. 'I won't.'

'There must be something out there that'll be a good balance.' He looked thoughtful, and then he smiled. 'Why are you looking so surprised?' he asked, his hand curving around his tall glass of iced water.

'Well—' Jemima searched for a way of expressing what she was feeling '—your mother…'

Miles shook his head. 'Hermione is Hermione. Her views are extreme and I've experienced the consequences of them.'

He must have. Everything he said about his childhood made her feel intensely sorry for him. 'Do you always call her Hermione?' she asked curiously after a moment.

He nodded, eating another mouthful of his pasta. 'Unless she irritates me especially. If she writes about me in her column and the ripples hit my life in any kind of negative way, then I find calling her Mum is very effective.

'The ultimate punishment, of course, will be to make her a grandmother. Although I'm sure she'd turn it to her advantage as long as I've not married the mother.' He smiled across at her. 'Do you want parmesan?'

It seemed an abrupt change of conversation, but clearly Miles was so used to his background that he expected other people to find it as easy to come to terms with. She didn't know quite what to say. His background was so different from hers.

Her mum delighted in her grandchildren, even more since her retirement. She was more of a hands-on grandmother than she'd ever had time to be as a mother.

'You look shocked.'

Jemima shook her head. 'Just can't quite imagine calling my mum "Margaret".' But it was more than that. In all the world there was only Ben and Sam who could call her 'Mum'. That made it special. *Didn't it?*

'Do you want parmesan?' Miles asked again.

She looked at it a little longingly. 'I mustn't.'

'Why ever not?'

Jemima looked at him as though he'd developed two heads. Every day of his working life he was surrounded by stick insects. He must have noticed the difference.

His eyes glinted and his voice was pure temptation. 'Parmesan is an essential. A staple of life. And
you've got to try the Apple and Vanilla Tart later.'
His mouth twisted into its almost habitual sexy
smile. 'It beats Alistair's fig concoction hands down
anyway.'

There was a brief moment during lunch where
she regretted her lack of willpower, but it was
shortlived when she tasted the tart. Jemima's lips
closed round the warm puff pastry base with its
sweet apple topping and she sighed. 'I'm never
going to be thin. I may as well accept it.'

Miles laughed, sitting back in his chair.

'Verity never eats desserts. I think they must be
against her religion,' she joked.

'Then she misses out. Try the ice cream with the
tart. The combination is terrific.'

Jemima didn't disagree. The cold and the warm
mingled in her mouth and she closed her eyes to
allow her sense of taste to fully experience it.

'Good?'

'Incredible.' She felt a little self-conscious as
she opened her eyes to find Miles was smiling at
her, almost laughing, but not unkindly.

'Why is it everything that's bad for you tastes
so good?' Jemima rushed on, unnerved by his expression. 'Verity eats everything with chopsticks.
She reckons she eats far less that way.'

'It's a cruel business she's in. Most models are

emaciated.' Then he looked up with an intensely wicked gleam in his eyes and Jemima braced herself for something shocking. 'Great with their clothes on, not so great without.'

Jemima sent him what her mum would describe as an 'old-fashioned look'. 'And you should know.'

His smile widened and it felt as if a million butterflies had been let loose in her stomach.

How did he do that? She'd forgotten what it was like to flirt and laugh for no reason. Truthfully, she'd forgotten what it was like to have fun. But sitting here in the summer sunshine, the noise and the bustle of Covent Garden going on all around…

She felt more like the woman she'd been when she'd first left university. Anything had seemed possible then.

Miles finished the last of his dessert and reached out for the notepad. 'It's very dull to go out with a woman who's watching every mouthful.'

'I watch every mouthful. The trouble is I'm eating it at the time.'

Miles laughed. 'But you didn't order salad with no dressing or some peculiar combination that's the latest craze. I hate that.'

'I must have tried every diet going.'

'Why?'

Why? Jemima mentally ran through the possible whys. On the BMI index she was coming in at the perfectly respectable top end of normal, but she still felt this…pressure to be thinner.

It was as though she believed her life would be better, happier, more successful, if only she looked…well, thinner.

And that pressure hadn't come from her family. Surprising, considering she had a super-model-sized sister. In the family they all thought Verity looked better a stone heavier.

It was *Russell*. It came as a shock to realise it was Russell's voice she heard in her head. Still. He'd been so keen for her to lose the 'baby weight' she'd gained. Perhaps because he'd already started to be unhappy living with her.

Jemima shrugged the bad memories away. Though some time she ought to think about it more. It made her angry to think she'd allowed Russell to control how she felt about herself.

Miles was reading down the list she'd started. Three weeks ago, if anyone had told her she'd be sitting in Covent Garden's beautiful glass-covered building with a man like Miles Kingsley she'd have laughed.

But here she was. And he didn't look desperately bored. He wasn't glancing down at his watch as Russell had used to do, or making her feel as though she had nothing to talk about but nappies and playschools.

Just possibly, Jemima thought with a new

stirring of anger, the problem was with Russell and not with her.

Miles looked up and surprised her watching him. 'Why don't we divide and conquer with all of this?' he said, gesturing down at the long 'To Do' list.

'How would it be if I leave you with tracking down a marquee since, frankly, I don't know where to start with it and searching out possible caterers? And I'll sort out the medieval musicians and the…florist. I might have some contacts that'll be useful,' he said and his eyes were smiling.

Jemima kept a straight face. 'I think ringing Becky is probably a great idea.'

'It'll give her heart failure if I tell her I'm choosing flowers for a wedding.'

'Scare her, more like. You must be ten per cent of her business.' Jemima started putting Rachel's clippings and tear sheets back into the box file. 'What are you going to do if your contacts aren't useful? Realistically, Becky can't do flowers for a wedding in Kent, can she?'

He smiled and she felt as though she'd swallowed something hard and spiky. 'If it all goes pear-shaped I'll call you to fix it.'

CHAPTER EIGHT

MILES flung his jacket across the sofa and sat, staring at the telephone as though it might speak and tell him what to do.

It had been a long and intensely dull evening. Keira Rye-Stanford was all glitz and no substance. She'd looked…amazing. There was no other way to describe her. Tall, elegant, sexy—and delighted to be out with him. So far, so good one would think.

Miles rubbed his hand across his aching neck. *Hell, he'd been bored.* There'd been moments when he'd wondered whether he'd manage to keep his eyes open long enough to end the evening politely.

Lunch with Jemima had felt like a five minute highlight of the day, whereas dinner with Keira had felt like a five hour endurance course.

And, when he looked at it logically, he didn't know *why*. Keira was a great idea, Jemima a dreadfully bad one.

Keira was an alluring, independently wealthy career woman who didn't have a genuinely romantic bone in her body. Jemima was 'walking wounded' from her divorce, had two dependent children and an irrational belief in living happily ever after.

Miles smoothed his hand across the taupe-coloured suede of his sofa and debated whether eleven was really too late to ring Jemima. He wanted her to know…

What?

He frowned. What was it that he wanted her to know? That he was home by eleven? That he was home alone?

He stretched back on the sofa and debated the wisdom of ringing her. All he needed was an excuse, some…reason for calling. His eyes lighted on the scribbled note he'd left on the coffee table and he reached for his phone. If she'd gone to bed she'd have switched her mobile off and he could leave a message for the morning. Safe enough.

Miles tapped in her number, so convinced she wouldn't answer, that he was surprised when she did. 'Jemima!'

'Yes.'

'Are you awake?' Miles closed his eyes. *Daft, daft question!* Of course, if she'd answered the phone she was awake. What kind of idiot was he?

'Miles?'

And she didn't even recognise his voice. It was getting better and better. 'Miles Kingsley.' He cleared his throat. *Damn!* He felt…like an adolescent schoolboy.

What was he trying to achieve here? Jemima didn't *need* to know he'd found a group of musicians who were prepared to play at the wedding. Not tonight.

It was merely his need to hear her voice that meant he had to call her. 'I've just got in and I thought I'd try and catch you before…'

Bed. Not a good thought. Miles thrust an agitated hand through his hair, his mind inevitably starting to imagine what Jemima might wear in bed. Seamlessly he went on to wonder whether her freckles covered every inch of her body. Or, more intriguingly, whether there were areas they didn't?

'…before you went to sleep,' he continued, his voice slightly deeper.

'I'm awake. I've just finished ironing all the school uniforms for Monday. How did your dandelion date go?'

How to answer that? Keira had worn a dress that was designed to make sure a man thought about what it would be like to take it off. She'd listened attentively to everything he said, had moistened her lips and tossed her hair. But, undeniably beautiful though Keira was, he hadn't been remotely tempted by her. He'd dropped her outside her

Chelsea house and walked away without a backward glance.

'No, don't tell me,' Jemima continued, without him needing to say anything. 'I can gauge it all by the type of flowers you get me to send her on Monday.'

Miles sat back on the sofa, hoping that a nonchalant posture would somehow transmute itself into his voice.

'Does she know that's the form?' Jemima asked. 'A cactus and it's all off, two dozen red roses and I'll need to buy a hat.'

Her voice was full of teasing laughter and he felt the boredom of his evening evaporate. Jemima did have the sexiest voice. It coated her words like warm chocolate over fruit. It relaxed him. *Seduced him.* 'Buy a hat?'

'For the wedding.'

'Ah,' he said, understanding. 'You know, I've never sent a woman a cactus—'

'Yet,' Jemima cut in swiftly.

Miles laughed, although there was a part of him that felt piqued. *Didn't it bother Jemima at all that he'd spent the evening with another woman?* And, if not, *why* not?

He'd spent the better part of the evening thinking about her. He'd wondered whether she'd told Ben and Sam about their trip into town. If she still felt sad at the thought of missing Ben's party. But, most of all, he'd wondered whether she was thinking about him at all…

Less than a minute into this phone call and it was crystal clear she hadn't given him a moment's consideration.

'A cactus isn't a very persuasive plant,' he said smoothly.

'And a dandelion is? Goodness, Miles, you know the wrong women.'

It was an opinion he was beginning to share. What would Jemima say if he asked her out to dinner—right now? This moment? The answer came swinging into his mind with the velocity of a cricket ball at the Oval. *She'd say no*. There wouldn't be a moment's hesitation.

If he asked Jemima out on a date he'd have his first slap-back since Jenny Baymen told him he couldn't take off her bra. He'd been fifteen then and his technique had lacked sophistication.

But…

Miles shifted his position on the sofa and made the conscious decision to make it clear that he had a real, bona fide reason for ringing her. Something that had absolutely nothing to do with the fact that he'd not been able to forget how green her eyes were or how pale her skin. Or that he remembered, absolutely, how it had felt to kiss her.

'I wouldn't rush to get the hat,' he said, uncomfortable and shifting his position yet again. *It had felt so good to kiss her.* It would be even better if he could kiss her when she was lying down beside him, warm and sleepy. If he could reach out and touch her...

'Not a good evening, then. How very disappointing, and after such a promising start.'

Women never teased him, Miles thought with a slow smile. If Jemima had asked him in for 'coffee' tonight he wouldn't have left her standing on the doorstep. He would have taken her inside and started a detailed exploration of just how far her freckles covered that pale, almost translucent, skin.

Miles shook his head, mystified by how he was feeling. *Jemima?* The intensity of it was frightening and entirely unexpected.

But the really tragic thing was that when Jemima asked him in for 'coffee' she really did mean coffee.

The truth was she was as unimpressed by him as he was by himself. For the first time in his adult life he felt as though he'd met a woman who could see past the façade—and she thought him shallow.

He sat forward and rested his elbows on his thighs. 'Whatever my evening was like, it was probably better than yours if you spent it looking through bridal magazines.'

She gave a rich chuckle. 'You've got me there. Did you know you can buy silver-plated yo-yos with the words 'you make my world go round' engraved on them?

'Actually, no.'

'Apparently it makes a great gift for a page-boy.'

'Would it?' he asked, marvelling at how steady his voice was.

'I can't see it either,' she agreed easily, 'but I've done brilliantly with the marquee. Or I think I have.'

Miles stood up with the phone tucked under his ear and walked across to the kitchen to fetch a beer from the fridge. 'I hope it's got turrets and a flag waving on the top or Rachel's going to be disappointed.'

'That's just it. It hasn't.'

Miles poured his beer into a tall glass and walked back to the sofa. 'What have you done?'

'Well, it suddenly occurred to me that the people who were to have had that weekend at Manningtree Castle had probably reserved something.

'While you were out of the office this afternoon, I did a bit of digging, found out who it was, and I've agreed to take over their booking. What do you think? Good idea?'

'Clever.' *No more than he expected from her.*

'It's large and white and we'll have to add the medieval touches ourselves, but it's a marquee and Alistair and Rachel are running out of time.'

'Now all you need to do is find a caterer who fancies roasting an entire pig over a spit.' Miles sat back and waited for her reaction.

'Don't you have contacts for that?' she asked silkily.

It was so good to be home. So good to be talking to Jemima. 'I know. It's such an odd place to have a huge gap in my address book.' Miles sipped his beer. 'But I have pulled all kinds of strings and pledged a ridiculous amount of money to Great Ormond Street Hospital in order to hire a group of baroque musicians called Solstice.'

'How did giving money to Great Ormond Street Hospital help?'

'You may well ask.' Miles pushed off his shoes and sat back more comfortably. 'One of the violinists is the daughter of a paediatrician who just happens to be the boyfriend of the sister of Hugh Foxton. And Alistair and I went to school with Hugh.'

There was a moment's stunned silence and then, 'Good grief!'

Miles laughed. 'Impressed?'

'Very.'

There was a momentary sense of exultation and then he realised that he no longer had an ostensible reason for speaking to her—and he wasn't ready for her to go yet. 'Have you spoken to your boys about tomorrow?' he asked abruptly.

'Not yet. I thought I'd make it a surprise, but I've already packed a picnic so we don't waste any time in the morning.'

Miles pictured a few rounds of sandwiches, the kind she brought into work each day tightly wrapped in cling film. Then he imagined Jemima and her boys struggling to find somewhere to eat them. In a just world she'd have been able to take them to a restaurant, money no object.

She seemed to take it all in her stride, but it angered him that she had to think like that. Pinching and scraping for every blasted thing while Russell wafted in and out of his sons' lives like Santa Claus bringing gifts.

'Have you planned your day?' he asked, frowning.

'Not really. I thought I'd see what the boys want to do. They might be happy enough wandering through the market.'

No. The thought burst within him. He wanted better than that for her. Better than a day left to chance with one eye on what everything cost. This had to be a fantastic day. A day that Jemima would love to give her boys.

The kind of day he'd missed out on himself. Where would be the harm in that? It wasn't as though he would be really involving himself in her family. But he could help her. She found his ability to network and the myriad contacts he had amusing, but one phone call…

Miles transferred the phone to his other ear. 'Jemima?'

'What?'

'If you don't have anything fixed for the afternoon I thought I might ring a couple of people and call in a favour or two.'

'Miles, I—'

He could hear the doubt in her voice. 'It's just an idea. I'll talk to you about it tomorrow.'

'You don't have to feel—'

He stopped her. 'Just concentrate your mind on finding someone who specialises in cooking over an open fire and I'll come up with something I think Ben will enjoy.'

And that was where it would stop, he promised silently. He needed to refocus on how impossible a relationship would be with Jemima. Only…it was becoming more and more difficult to remember that.

'Do you really work here, Mum?' Sam asked the following morning, pushing his face close to the glass entrance doors of Kingsley and Bressington.

'Yes. You'll see where in a minute.' Jemima pulled him back and nervously touched her wildly curling hair. She should have straightened it like normal. She only hoped Miles wouldn't think she'd left it curly because he'd said he thought it looked sexy.

Although she had. Obviously. Which was sort of fine as long as it wasn't *obvious* to him that she had.

'There's a man coming,' Ben said, standing to one side of her.

Sam pressed forward. 'That's Miles. I went in his car when I was sick.'

Jemima felt her stomach clench. She was being ridiculous, but her mouth was dry and her hands clammy as she watched him walk towards the doors, effortlessly sexy in denim jeans and blue T-shirt.

Her reaction to him was as instant as a puppet's to the jerking of its strings. Jemima smoothed down her fitted cotton blouse and tucked her hands into the pockets of her own jeans. *Heaven help her.*

'Hi,' she said breathlessly as he opened the door for them to come in.

'Hi yourself.' And for a moment Miles looked at her.

She felt more self-conscious in that moment than she'd done in her entire life. Every instinct was to fluff her hair and hold her stomach muscles in tight. *What was he seeing when he looked at her like that?*

Then he turned away. 'So, you must be Ben,' he said with an easy smile in her son's direction. 'I've already met Sam.'

'I went in his car,' the younger boy chirped in, his grin wide and toothless.

Jemima placed a hand on Sam's head and steered

them inside. Ben looked round, clearly overawed by the dramatic interior.

'Cool,' he said, looking at the staircase that seemed to float upwards. 'This is so much cooler than Dad's office.'

Above his head Miles met Jemima's eyes and smiled. 'You'd better see where your mum is working. It's upstairs.'

Sam slipped his hand inside hers as Jemima led them towards her temporary office. She was aware of Miles shutting and locking the door before he followed on behind.

'I work through here,' Jemima said, showing the boys the stunning interior of her office.

Ben's eyes instantly focused on the computer as she'd known they would. 'Does it have games on it?' he asked.

Jemima caught Miles's soft laugh. 'I shouldn't think so. I haven't had time to play games while I've been here.'

'Mine does,' Miles interrupted and she turned round to look at him. He grinned unrepentantly and walked over to open the door to his office. 'Do you want a go?'

Neither Ben or Sam needed to be asked a second time. They lost all sense of nervousness as they realised that they'd finally come into contact with a grown-up who knew that, *of course*, they'd want to have a go.

Jemima watched as the three male heads crowded round the screen. Then Miles looked up and smiled at her and she felt breathless again.

She stepped back into the comparative safety of her own office, trying to remember all the reasons why she would never be able to trust any man ever again. And, most particularly, why she couldn't trust this one.

'They're quick on the uptake,' Miles said as he joined her.

'Yes.' Jemima rubbed her hands down the legs of jeans. 'I think it's something they're born with these days. Ben seems to know instinctively how to work my mobile phone better than I do and I've spent ages reading the instructions.'

Silently Jemima counted to ten. She had to keep a perspective on things. It was only because it was a Saturday and the Kingsley and Bressington building was empty that it felt so strange.

Miles was just being kind.

'Tea? Coffee?' Miles asked as he walked over to the kitchen. There was nothing different about him. He still looked as though he was completely comfortable and in control of his world. The difficulty was with her.

'Um.'

He smiled at her. 'I think they may be a while.'

'Yes. Sorry.' She took another deep breath. *Oh, stuff it!* This was horrible. 'Were you working? I can call them off any time and you can get on…'

'It's fine. I've done everything I need to do today.'

Which naturally made her worry he'd been hanging round waiting for them to arrive when he really wanted to get off home. *She just wasn't good at this*. Whatever *this* was.

She followed Miles into the small kitchen. 'I can't believe you have games on your computer,' she said, struggling for normality.

He laughed.

'So when you've been shut away in there and I thought you were working you've actually been trying to increase your top score?'

Miles winked at her and her stomach flipped over. 'Tea or coffee?'

She pulled one twist of hair straight in a nervous gesture she'd had since childhood. 'Coffee. Please.'

'Nice hair, by the way,' Miles remarked, turning to lean on the worktop. 'Very…sexy.' And his voice deepened in a way that made her believe he might really find it sexy.

Jemima could feel the blush spread across her face. She felt as if she was going to combust. What was happening here? Was it her? Or him?

'It's lovely.'

'Th-thank you.'

And then he reached out and touched one copper

corkscrew. Jemima stood motionless, her heart hammering against her chest as though it were contained in far too small a space. She couldn't breathe. She couldn't think.

There must be some smart clever comment she could say in a situation like this. Something light and sophisticated, but for the life of her Jemima couldn't think of it. She looked up helplessly into his eyes, eyes that had become impossibly dark.

All those clichés she'd read in books became instantly understandable. His eyes really *were* like two deep pools you could drown in. It all made perfect sense.

Flashes of what it had felt like when he'd kissed her played across her mind. Was she imagining it now, or was he looking at her as though he might do it again?

She felt scared and excited by it. She wanted him to kiss her. She didn't want him to kiss her. Her indecision lasted as long as the possibility.

Very, very slowly Miles let his hand fall to his side and he turned away, concentrating on making the coffee. Jemima felt as though she'd been sluiced in ice-cold water. He'd deliberately backed away from her and it felt like a rejection.

'I received an email from Alistair this morning.'

Jemima swallowed hard, trying to dislodge the hard lump stuck in her throat. 'Did you?'

'You can read it yourself, but...' Miles broke off

to pour the coffee into two mugs '…it seems everything is looking better than it did.'

'That's…great.'

'Alistair asked me to let you know. I don't know why he couldn't have sent it through to you directly—'

'M-my computer's not working at the moment.'

'Ah.'

Miles handed her a mug of coffee. 'Thanks.'

'I'm a bit muddled as to what is actually going on,' he said, pausing to take a sip of his own, 'but Alistair's dad is about to have, or has just had, an operation to remove a small tumour.'

Concentrating on what Miles was saying helped to calm her. She was reading far too much into what had been a casual gesture. Jemima followed him back out into her office and sat opposite him on one of the chairs. 'Is that connected to the haemorrhage or something different?'

'You'll need to read the email yourself. It was obviously dashed off in a hurry, but I think so. I think the tumour hit the artery—which could turn out to be a good thing, I suppose, if it means they can cut it out before it's had a chance to spread.'

In the nearby office there was a loud cheer. 'They seem happy,' Miles remarked.

'Yes.' Jemima made a huge effort to relax. 'They loved the tube ride in as well. I probably don't really need to do anything else.'

Miles put his mug down on the shattered glass coffee table. 'I forgot. I've arranged something for your afternoon. I only hope Ben will like it. I don't have much experience of nine-year-old boys.'

'Except having been one yourself.'

'Except having been one myself,' he echoed, turning back to her with a warm expression in his eyes. It made her feel unaccountably shy, all the more so when he handed across a plain white envelope. 'I think I'd have liked this.'

'What is it?' Jemima asked, holding out the envelope.

'Open it.'

With one more questioning glance, Jemima flicked open the unsealed envelope and looked down at tickets for a Thames river cruise and... 'What's this?' she asked, looking across at him, bemused.

'I've hired a private capsule on the London Eye.'

'Yes, I know, but—'

'It means you have a capsule to yourself and priority boarding. That's one thing I do remember about being nine. I hated having to stand in line waiting for things.' He smiled. 'Actually I've not changed much. I still hate waiting.'

Jemima didn't know whether she ought to cry or to laugh. She didn't know whether she ought to accept it either.

She'd looked at tickets for the London Eye

months ago and decided it really was too pricey. How much had Miles had to pay to get a private capsule?

Miles pulled a hand through his hair and stood up as though he sensed her indecision. 'Hopefully I've timed it right so you've still got time to have your lunch.'

'Thank you.' Jemima carefully folded the tickets and put them back in the envelope.

'It's a shame we didn't think about it earlier because Ben could have asked some of his school friends along. You can have up to twenty-five guests, I think—'

'Miles.' She stopped him and he turned to look at her. Jemima held the envelope out helplessly as though she didn't quite know what to do with it. 'This is lovely, but…how much did this cost you? I really didn't mean you to—'

'I told you, I was owed a favour. It's nothing.'

'But—'

'And anyway, it's not for you, it's for Ben's birthday. Just have a good time.'

Miles turned away as though what he'd done for them was completely insignificant. *But it wasn't.* It really wasn't.

Inside her head sparks were flying. She wasn't sure what she thought about anything any more. What she was thinking had to be *impossible*.

But then she thought about the way his eyes had

darkened when they'd looked at her earlier. The way she'd been so sure he was about to kiss her.

What did any of it mean? She was so out of practice at reading the signals. And she'd hardly ever been *in* practice. Russell had been her first serious boyfriend and he'd been more in love with the success of her family than her.

A man like Miles Kingsley? Attracted to her? It wasn't possible.

'Mum?'

Jemima turned to look at Ben standing in the doorway. 'There's a wicked picture of a sailing boat on this computer.'

She turned automatically to look at Miles.

He was looking at Ben. 'It a Najad. Forty-six foot. Swedish.'

'Is it yours?' Ben wanted to know.

Miles laughed. 'I wish. One day, perhaps. Are you interested in sailing?'

A shadow passed across Ben's face. 'I used to be, when I was a bit younger. We had a Heron, but Stefanie doesn't like sailing and Dad sold it.'

'Stefanie's your dad's girlfriend, right?'

Ben nodded.

'Perhaps you'd come out with me in my dinghy? You know, some time? If your mum's happy with that.' He looked across at her.

Jemima thought she wanted to cry, but when she looked at Ben's face she knew she wasn't going to. She didn't understand why Miles would do that for Ben, but she was absolutely sure she could trust him not to carelessly hurt her son. She didn't know how she knew that for certain either, she just did.

Jemima looked at Miles. 'Come with us today?' Then she hesitated, amazed she'd found the courage to ask him. 'I…I mean, if you're not too busy this afternoon, that is.'

Oh, help.

Miles started to shake his head so she rushed on, 'It seems a shame for just the three of us to go on if there's space for twenty-five.'

Jemima felt as though her face must be shining with embarrassment. It was almost as though she'd asked him out. She wanted to curl up into a ball. He must be so embarrassed. He'd tried to be kind and she'd completely got the wrong end of the stick and…

'On one condition.'

Jemima looked up at him. Slowly he smiled and her mortification faded. 'I get to buy you lunch.'

Lunch? Whatever she'd thought he'd say, it hadn't been that. 'You'll come with us to use tickets you got us,' she said slowly, 'as long as I let you buy us all lunch?'

'That's about it. Do we have a deal?'

'We've brought…' *sandwiches*, she finished mentally. What was the matter with her? The lines

at the edges of his blue eyes deepened and she fell
that little bit more under his spell. 'We'd like that.'

What was it he wanted from her? They were
such *different* people. She had to be imagining
what she thought he was thinking. *But what if she
wasn't?*

Miles had a philosophy of life that was completely incompatible with hers. She couldn't
change—and, she suspected, neither could he. But
there were these moments when he looked at her
when all those differences didn't seem to be very
important.

It was so daft. Miles dated amazing women.
Women as beautiful as Verity, as confident as
Imogen and as successful as her mother. It was
inconceivable...

She couldn't even put words on the idea that had
taken up residence in her head. Why would Miles
be attracted to someone as...*normal* as her?

CHAPTER NINE

'Mum, isn't pepperoni the best topping on pizza?' Ben asked, bringing Jemima back into the concrete present. 'Miles says it's beef and chilli—'

Miles winked at her. 'Or ham and pineapple. Everyone loves that.'

'Mum,' her boys said in unison, stretching that one syllable into something with at least three. 'Tell him it's pepperoni.'

Jemima sat back, a smile tugging at her mouth. She couldn't remember the last time she'd taken the boys out to eat anywhere. It was just too expensive. She knew that Russell did it fairly regularly, whenever Stefanie wanted some peace and quiet, but…this was such a rare occurrence for her—and it was all the more special for that.

Special, too, because Miles was there to share it with her. He made everything seem easy somehow. For a man who hadn't had much contact with children, and claimed not to want it, he made it look effortless.

Miles looked over the top of his menu at her, the expression in his eyes making her feel as though she were entirely composed of marshmallow.

'It's going to have to be your decision,' Miles said. 'But I want you to know I fully intend to bear a grudge if you decide against me.'

Jemima laughed as her sons immediately started canvassing for her vote.

'Why don't we have the one that's got a mixture of toppings on it?' she suggested, her negotiating skills honed by experience. 'Then we can try a bit of all of them and give them a mark out of ten.'

'Like a cake picnic,' Ben said.

Miles lifted an eyebrow in her direction. 'What's a cake picnic?' he asked.

The boys fell over themselves to tell him. Ben leant forward eagerly. 'We choose a cake each and cut it into three bits—'

'It's cool,' Sam said with a wide toothless smile. 'You get a bit of all of them.'

'Mum always picks shortbread.'

Miles looked across at her and his eyes were laughing. 'Does she?'

'Particularly if it's been dipped in chocolate,' Jemima agreed, keeping a straight face. 'And Ben always has a chocolate éclair.'

'And the cream drops down his top,' Sam said, 'because he doesn't lean over the plate.'

Ben looked stormy, but Miles forestalled world war three with a quick, 'Okay, I get it. Pizza picnic it is.' Then he folded the menu and asked the boys, 'Who wants what to drink?'

Ben looked at his mum for guidance.

Miles also turned to her and she tried to answer as nonchalantly as possible. 'We tend to either have something to eat and ask for tap water, or we have a drink and nothing to eat.'

This was where people usually said something sympathetic—and made her feel worse about it. When they were with their father, she knew, Ben and Sam could have anything they wanted.

Miles said simply, 'Sounds like a good plan.' Then he smiled and looked at her. 'But…since this is a special occasion. What do you think?'

Jemima swallowed hard. 'I—It's your money,' she managed.

When the waiter brought across a tall glass with Coke in it, Ben couldn't quite believe his luck. 'This is the best birthday treat ever,' he said and his younger brother nodded in full agreement.

'Well, it's not often you get to be nine. In fact,' Miles said, 'I've only done it once.'

Ben and Sam dissolved into giggles—and it was a state Miles pretty much kept them in.

Jemima enjoyed watching them. *All of them.*

And she found she could relax. For the first time since Russell had decided to walk out on their marriage, she wasn't totally responsible for the success of the day. Of course, she *was* responsible. She knew that. They were her children.

But it was different with Miles there. Better. *Much better.*

When he suggested they walk to the London Eye rather than take the tube, she didn't have to worry about working out the route in her A-Z. She merely had to follow, confident that when he led them down tiny side roads Miles knew exactly where he was going.

It might not sound like much, but it *felt* revolutionary. Sam had been only two and a half when Russell had decided to leave and, from that moment, Jemima had been 'it'. Every sleepless night, every illness, every decision she'd made for them had been her responsibility alone.

'Did you know,' Miles said, as they boarded their capsule, 'that one thousand, seven hundred tonnes of steel was used to construct the Eye?'

Ben and Sam looked at him.

'Which means it's heavier than two hundred and fifty double-decker buses…and can carry fifteen thousand visitors every day, which is more than enough to fill Concorde one hundred and sixty times over.'

The boys were suitably amazed. So was she, but

for very different reasons. Miles was so…unexpected.

How had he guessed that Ben loved facts and figures? That his favourite reading was the kind of huge tome crammed full of a thousand and one things no one else knew and probably wouldn't need to. Jemima smiled. Miles had set out to make this day magical for Ben and he was doing just that. It was also magical for her.

Sam came and tucked his hand into hers as they started to climb higher, but Ben was peering out of the glass from the very beginning.

'Why do they call it a flight?' he asked Miles and she tried not to laugh as her usually articulate boss did his best to answer to the satisfaction of a nearly-nine-year-old.

Strange, but she didn't think of him as her boss any more. Their relationship had changed irrevocably since dinner with Alistair and Rachel. Jemima turned on the bench to look at him, watching the way his T-shirt stretched over his toned torso. *Heart-stoppingly handsome*, she thought—and way, way out of her league. But there were moments when he looked at her when she was sure…

Her smile twisted. Even if she had done all those abdominal crunches after Sam was born, how attractive would she really be to a man like Miles who had his pick of women? It didn't seem particularly likely and, truth be told, she wouldn't be happy in the kind of relationship Miles advocated.

She was naturally monogamous, she supposed. She wanted to build 'family' and make things secure for the people she loved. *Was that so wrong?*

As Sam ventured over to join his brother, Miles came to sit beside her on the wooden seating. 'Good idea?' he asked, his eyes indicating the glass capsule they were in. 'Do you think they're enjoying it?'

Jemima couldn't believe he was experiencing a moment of doubt about it, but his blue eyes seemed to be waiting for an answer. 'It's brilliant. They're loving it. Thank you.'

Then he smiled and she wondered whether it was doing her heart any permanent damage to keep beating so erratically. For thirty years she hadn't experienced the slightest difficulty, but since meeting Miles it had been behaving very peculiarly.

'Are you?'

She nodded, feeling unaccountably shy.

'Come see,' he said, holding out his hand.

Slowly, her heart pounding, Jemima put her hand inside his. She'd seen a movie once where they'd talked about looking down and not knowing where one hand left off and the other began. It felt a little like that, except that she knew which hand belonged to whom. His hand was dark against her fair skin. It was more that she felt as if it belonged there.

Jemima tried to pretend that nothing had changed, but she was too honest a person not to know she was falling in love with Miles. Little by little. Despite the paralysing fear of being hurt again, she knew she was sliding inexorably closer to the point where there would be no way back.

She didn't want to be in love with him. *Or did she?* Surely at thirty the idea of giving way to unrequited passion, particularly when you were responsible for two young lives, was a bit ridiculous. And, if it wasn't unrequited, what then?

What was Miles thinking? She looked up at him, trying to read what was going on in his head. It seemed so…*unlikely* that he should be feeling anything like she was.

But there *was* that look in his eyes—just sometimes. The expression that made her feel hot and cold at the same time. Excited and scared.

And now he was holding her hand. Miles led her over to where she had a perfect view of the River Thames snaking through the city. It was an amazing thing to see, curiously beautiful and everything it was hyped up to be, but it was the feel of his fingers interlocked with hers that filled her senses.

'There's Buckingham Palace,' Miles said, pointing.

Jemima took a shaky breath. 'There's so much green around it,' was the only thing she could think of to say in reply.

She felt him smile. 'Not a bad back garden,' Miles agreed.

'It's amazing to see the whole city laid out like this,' she said, conscious of the fact that he was still holding her hand. There was no reason for him to be holding it, other than that he wanted to.

Did he want to?

'Have you been on the Eye before?'

She shook her head. 'I thought it would be a little like the Ferris wheel in Vienna, but it feels so different…' Then she stopped as a memory started to ache like an old wound.

She didn't want to think about that. Not now. It was years since she'd been in Vienna with Russell. She didn't want to think of him now.

'Bad memories?' Miles asked, watching her face.

Her mouth twisted. 'Actually, no. Good memories turned bad.'

'Difficult to forget?'

'You can never forget,' she said brusquely. 'I know I've been divorced a year and everyone seems to think I should be over it by now, but no one *gets over* something like that. It's such a stupid thing to say. You can't just erase all the memories and pretend none of it happened.'

Jemima made a half-hearted effort to take back her hand, but Miles refused to let her pull away. 'Do you…still love him?'

'No,' she said quickly and then, more slowly, 'No, I don't, but I did.' Her eyes searched for understanding. 'And…he's the father of my children. It's not as though I can draw a line beneath the whole experience and re-invent myself.'

Miles moved his thumb gently across the palm of her hand, sympathetic and erotic at the same time.

'When you've been…badly let down by someone you trusted, it's always inside you. You think you're fine and then something happens and you…remember.'

'Like now?'

Jemima shrugged. 'Russell proposed to me in Vienna.' *She shouldn't be saying all this*. Not to Miles. Everyone said that the first rule of 'getting back out there' was that you never talked about your failed relationships…

But what if you hadn't had so many failed relationships? What if there'd only been the one? And what if it had been the largest part of your adult life? *How was it possible not to talk about it?* Almost every memory she had since the age of eighteen involved Russell or Russell's children.

Miles was frowning.

'He proposed on the Ferris wheel?'

'In a felucca,' she said with a shake of her head. 'It's a horse-drawn carriage.'

'Yes, I know.'

'It was supposed to be very romantic because I'd really wanted to go in one, but—' and she bit down on a laugh as she remembered the farcical elements of the ride '—it started to rain halfway round and we had to stop while the driver put the hood up.'

The frown disappeared from his forehead. 'Probably an omen.' Then he reached out and slowly, very slowly, stroked her cheek. Jemima felt her breath freeze. The felucca hadn't been romantic—but this was. This was incredible. It was the kind of thing that only happened to other people.

'I'd like to kiss you,' Miles said quietly. So quietly she was almost unsure of what she'd heard.

'W-would you?' Her voice sounded cracked and dry.

'You're beautiful.' She shook her head in denial and he smiled. His hand moved so that his thumb could lightly brush against her lips. 'Why do you find that so surprising?'

Jemima could have recited all the things Russell had filled her head with when he'd wanted to justify his decision to leave. Miles couldn't have noticed that she was focused entirely on her children, that she wasn't spontaneous and that she took life too seriously.

Miles smiled and pushed back a red curl from her forehead. 'I need to bring you back here. You ought to see London when it's lit by electric light.'

A date? Was that what he was meaning? Jemima swallowed nervously. Miles *was* attracted to her. She wasn't imagining it. The air thinned around her and she struggled to think of anything beyond that.

'Look, Mum,' Ben said from the other side of the capsule. 'Look down here.'

Miles let his hand drop and Jemima walked over to look where her eldest son was pointing. Far below on the ground there was a clown with exceptionally long arms and big white hands.

Sam pushed his face up against the glass and peered down. 'He looks funny.'

'Yes,' she agreed, looking up to catch Miles watching her. A *frisson* of awareness passed between them. It was really happening.

And he wanted to kiss her. That thought stayed swirling around in her head—exciting and scary at the same time. *Miles* wanted to kiss her.

She was aware of everything he said, everywhere he moved. She noticed the way he rested a hand on Ben's shoulder as they stepped out of the capsule, exactly as she might have done herself. Ben normally would have shrugged someone he didn't know well off. But he'd looked up and smiled. Miles couldn't know the incredible compliment he'd been paid. But she knew.

She thought about that as the four of them walked towards the pier and watched the boat dock that was to take them on their river cruise. She felt Miles inadvertently brush against her and glanced up at him. He smiled and there was nothing she could do but smile back. She felt as if she was in freefall.

Jemima knew she only took in a fraction of the sights. Somewhere amongst all her memories of the day was Miles's voice pointing out the famous landmarks as they passed and her boys' excited questions.

'That's the Houses of Parliament.'

'Why does it have green striped blinds and red striped blinds?' Ben wanted to know. 'Is it because they ran out of material?'

Sam yawned and sat down next to Miles. Without thinking, Miles stretched out his arm and tucked the young boy in close. 'Tired?'

'I'm never tired.'

Jemima watched her son instinctively curve into Miles. *How had he managed to get them to trust him like that?* In the space of one afternoon he'd absorbed himself into her family, made them trust him. Made *her* trust him.

Slowly Sam's eyes closed and Miles looked across at her. 'He's tired.'

Jemima nodded. 'We'd better start for home. It'll be quite late by the time we get back.'

'The tube's not far from here.'

This incredible day was over.

As they approached the pier, Jemima reached down and picked up her backpack, still full of the uneaten sandwiches. Miles took it off her. 'I'll walk with you to the tube.'

Jemima said nothing. She didn't quite trust her voice and wasn't sure what she'd say anyway. Her mind was one large exclamation mark. She needed time to think and to consider what was happening. She couldn't quite believe…

Why would Miles Kingsley…?

'Ben—' she called her son, who was staring up at the London Eye '—keep with us.'

'Sam's got his energy back,' Miles observed seconds later, a smile in his voice.

Away from the gentle motion of the boat, Sam seemed to be back to a full quota of energy. 'Yes.'

The two boys ran slightly ahead, stopping every now and again to point something out or, rather less pleasantly, pick something up off the pavement. By the time they reached the tube station, Ben was fifty-two pence better off and Sam thirty-one pence from all the loose change they'd collected from the ground.

Jemima stopped. 'Thank you,' she began awkwardly. 'For today. It was…'

Miles stopped her with a gentle touch on her mouth. 'You're welcome.' His smile twisted and

Miles turned to look at Ben. 'Happy birthday. Thank you for letting me share your day with you.'

Ben came closer, hesitant suddenly. 'Will you really take me sailing?'

'If your mum is happy with that,' Miles said, with a glance up at her. 'We'll arrange something.'

His eyes were the blue of the darkest midnight sky and, Jemima thought, if this one moment was all there was it would be enough. *Almost*. And with that thought came the realisation that it was too late to be cautious. She already loved him. She loved him—and if she continued the way she was, she was about to get very hurt.

Miles put the phone down with mixed feelings. Of course it was great news that Alistair's dad was doing so well and that his doctors were confident they'd successfully removed the tumour. Alistair had sounded buoyant, a complete contrast to how he'd sounded a week ago.

It was great, too, that Rachel would be flying back to the UK immediately. Excellent. He frowned and walked over to look down on the street below. With a mere nine weeks to go before the wedding it was just as well. He and Jemima had performed miracles, but he would be pleased to hand the organisation of it back to the bride herself.

He didn't like weddings. Had never liked them. Miles pulled a tired hand across the back of his neck. So *why* did he feel this sense of disappointment?

It didn't take much introspection before he knew the answer to that. With Rachel back holding the reins, he'd no longer have any excuse to persuade Jemima out to lunch. *Damn.* If the woman wasn't interested, she wasn't interested. What was the matter with him?

He knew the answer to that too. In the space of a month Jemima had altered everything. He wasn't quite sure how; he just knew that she had. And he was fairly certain it wasn't that she wasn't interested, it was more she was running scared.

Miles walked across to the connecting door and looked across at Jemima's empty desk, then at the clock. She'd taken a late lunch, had slipped out while he'd been out of the office himself. By the time she returned he'd be out at meetings. All, he was sure, quite deliberate.

He turned back to sit at his desk, his fingers idly playing with the paper-clips. Jemima wanted the promise of 'for ever'—and he couldn't say that. He didn't see how anyone could. He made a rapid calculation. Suppose he lived until he was eighty. Quite possibly longer, given modern health care. That meant a conservative estimate of forty-four years. *Forty-four* years with one person. It wasn't *possible*.

He wasn't prepared to make Jemima promises

he knew he couldn't keep, but neither was he contemplating something temporary either. Jemima could set the pace. He had no problem with that—or, at least, not much.

Miles stood up and picked up his briefcase. What he was offering was a completely open-ended relationship. They could share their lives as long as it made them happy. He frowned. But Jemima had two boys in tow and how that fitted in with his unwillingness to risk becoming important in a child's life he wasn't quite sure. The emotional pull of his own childhood memories made him uncomfortable. But then, even if his relationship with Jemima finished, it didn't mean he need drop all contact with her children. He would be responsible…

Miles opened the connecting door and was startled to see Jemima. It was as though every time he saw her he was a little stunned by his reaction to her.

She turned. 'I thought you'd be gone. You'll be late for your meeting.'

Her hand moved to tug at a copper curl, then coiled it round her forefinger. Miles felt a smile tug at his mouth as he recognised the outward sign that she wasn't comfortable around him. There was some satisfaction in that.

'Alistair phoned.'

'I—I know. I mean I've spoken to Rachel and she told me about Alistair's dad. She rang while I was at lunch.' Jemima shut the door of the cupboard and went to sit at her desk. 'It's good news, isn't it?' she said brightly. A little too brightly, perhaps?

Miles nodded, watching her. 'Sounds like it. Although I doubt he'll make it over here for his son's wedding. I doubt they'd let him fly even if he felt up to it.'

'No.'

Miles shifted the grip of his briefcase. 'Did Rachel say what time she's expecting to get back to the UK?'

'I don't think she knows yet. She plans to get the first available flight.'

Which meant tomorrow was still an opportunity for him. Ben and Sam were with Russell. It was Ben's birthday, so Jemima wouldn't want to be alone. 'Shall we drive down to Manningtree Castle tomorrow?' he asked as casually as he could. 'Take the last opportunity to check everything we've arranged is going to work in that setting. Besides, I've still not seen it and I'm curious.'

Jemima bent down to pull a file out of the bottom drawer of her desk. 'I'm sorry. I've said I'll drive over to Rachel's as soon as the boys have left. She's desperate to know what we've done.'

'Right.' Miles smiled, if not easily, at least with the appearance of it. Some sixth sense told him he had to take the pressure off. Take it slowly. Inch by inch… 'It's a pity because we could have stopped off for a pub lunch somewhere, but I'm glad you're not planning on spending the day alone.'

She looked up and bit her lip.

He might be imagining it, but Miles wondered whether part of her was already regretting turning him down. He certainly hoped so. 'Wish Ben a happy birthday for me.'

'Yes. Yes, I will.'

Miles opened the door to leave. 'Have a good weekend.'

'You, too.'

He closed the door softly behind him. Miles smiled. Next weekend would be different. He'd take Ben sailing, perhaps invite Jemima and Sam to join them at the club later. There were possibilities.

Ben was good, Miles thought, watching the boy duck down without being warned as the boom swung across after a jibe. He enjoyed his company. Genuinely. He enjoyed teaching someone to sail who was so receptive.

And he liked knowing Ben's mother was on the bank. Miles looked into the distance and saw Jemima sitting on a bench watching them. Her hand was raised to shade her eyes from the sun.

'Perhaps it's time we headed back,' he suggested to Ben.

'Do we have to?'

'We can come again—' Miles smiled and knew

he meant it '—but I'm getting hungry and we've got to pack the boat away and have a shower before we can have our picnic.'

'Mum's made tuna rolls.' Ben shifted on the seat. 'And we've got lemon drizzle cake.'

It sounded perfect. Bizarrely. It was beginning to feel like a privilege to join their tightly knit circle. Who was he kidding? It *was* a privilege. A chance to experience the kind of family life he'd wanted as a child.

Miles turned the boat into the wind and zigzagged his way back to the bank. Jemima was on her feet immediately, her hand holding on to Sam's and one arm lightly resting on his shoulder as they waited.

'Mum,' Ben called out, 'I did better than last time. Did you see us nearly go over?'

The summer breeze caught at her curls and Jemima reached up to push them away. 'I saw.' Then she looked at Miles and smiled, intimate and warm, and he felt as if he was going over himself.

He *cared* about her. His smile twisted. That was rather a revolutionary concept for him. He wasn't sure he had ever cared about anyone before. At least not so it was uncomfortable for him. But he cared about Jemima. And he cared about the people she loved because she loved them.

'Can Sam help sponge down the insides?' Ben wanted to know.

Jemima shook her head. 'I want Sam to help me

set the picnic out.' She smiled again at Miles. 'We'll get everything out of the car and meet you at the tables. Over there.' She pointed towards the cluster of picnic tables on the other side of the lake. 'Is that okay?'

It was more than okay, Miles thought. It was great. He tried hard not to watch Jemima walk away. He didn't want Ben to notice how much he enjoyed seeing the way the filmy fabric of her summer dress blew about her legs.

'I've taken the bungs out,' Ben said, bringing him back to earth with a vengeance.

'Good.'

'Can we come sailing next Sunday?'

Miles shook his head. 'You're with your dad, but the weekend after that—if your mum is okay with it.'

By all that was reasonable the prospect of taking a nine-year-old sailing every other weekend should have had him hurrying in the opposite direction. Miles smiled, knowing he wouldn't change these Sundays for anything.

'Let's hurry up and get our showers. I'm hungry.'

'Mum won't let Sam eat all the crisps,' Ben observed. 'We need to put everything away properly.'

Miles laughed. Together they pulled the boat into position and put the sails into the sail bag. Then, when it was neatly covered, they walked towards the shower block.

By the time they'd arrived at the picnic tables Jemima had laid everything out. 'Do you want a coffee?' she asked as he approached, lifting up a flask. 'I've remembered to leave it black this time.'

Miles took the bench opposite her. That way he could watch the expressions that passed over her face. 'Thanks.'

She poured it into a plastic mug and handed it across to him with the kind of smile that had the blood pounding in his head.

'Miles, do you think dogs go to heaven?' Sam asked beside him. 'Mrs Randall says that dogs do, but goldfish don't—'

'Sit down to eat your sandwich, Sam,' Jemima instructed, passing Miles a plate. 'Ben, please eat a roll before you start on the crisps.'

Miles sat back and enjoyed it all. He loved this…the opportunity to be part of a family. *Jemima's family*. Somehow he'd become interested in every aspect of Jemima's life. In her boys. In her worries.

He loved her shy smile. The unexpected laughter that lit her green eyes. He loved the way she pulled at her hair when she was nervous. The way she smiled at him as though they were part of an exclusive world.

In fact, he couldn't remember ever feeling more…content.

Rachel sat on one of the bar stools in Jemima's kitchen, the list of things to check in the last two weeks before the wedding in front of her and her hands cradling a mug of hot coffee. 'So, let me get this straight,' she began incredulously.

Jemima turned to look at her, comfortably resting her back on the worktop.

'Miles has taken Ben sailing *three* times since I got back from Canada.'

'Four, if you count today,' Jemima said with a glimmer of laughter. 'Every other weekend.'

Rachel's eyebrows almost disappeared up into her hairline. She shook her head in disbelief. 'In a little dinghy?'

'I don't know much about sailing, but Ben says it's called a Heron. I think that's what Russell had, so I expect he's right.'

'On a little lake?'

Jemima smiled. 'It's quite a big lake.'

'Miles doesn't do lakes.' She shook her head. 'He's a serious sailor. He goes down Chichester way and sails over to France for lunch. You don't honestly believe he's doing it simply because he likes Ben, do you?'

'He's a friend—'

'Miles doesn't do *just friends* either. Come on, Jemima, you're divorced, not brain-dead.'

Jemima put her mug down on the worktop. 'I know he likes me—'

'Yes, he *likes* you. He also raises the temperature of a room just by looking at you.'

Jemima shook her head. 'That's nonsense.'

'So—' Rachel took a sip of coffee '—why do you think he bothered to introduce you to that literary scout?'

'Because Eileen was overloaded with work and was looking for someone who could read and write a report on what they'd read quickly. Miles knew I'd like to work from home. There's nothing odd about that.'

Rachel gave a despairing squawk. 'And you don't think it's because he fancies the pants off you?'

'A little. Maybe,' she conceded.

'*Maybe?*'

'Rachel, what do you expect me to do?' Jemima asked, finally irritated. 'I don't do affairs. I've *never* done affairs. I met Russell when I was eighteen and he's the only man I've ever slept with.'

'Slime-ball,' her friend interjected loyally.

'I've got two children to look after. I'm not about to jump into bed with a man like Miles. Am I?' she asked, picking up her empty mug and walking across to the dishwasher.

'Why not?'

Jemima stopped, turning to look at Rachel. 'Why not?' she repeated incredulously. 'Because I don't *do* that kind of thing.'

'You mean you *haven't* done that kind of thing,' Rachel corrected. She held up a hand. 'I know Miles isn't a great long-term bet, but he's…fun.'

'Fun,' Jemima repeated.

'And I'm not suggesting you make a habit of leaping into bed with men because they're fun, but I reckon Miles is just what you need right now. He's clever, sexy-looking, not going to take the whole thing too seriously… Fun.'

Fun. Jemima was sure that 'fun' was exactly how Miles saw it as well. And she was tempted. Of course she was tempted.

But…

She didn't understand affairs. Sex shouldn't be something casual. *Should it?* It had to mean something. What was so wrong with wanting to make a commitment to one man and to spend the rest of your life with him?

And that was the point, really. She was in love with Miles. Even Rachel would admit that beginning an affair with Miles if you were in love with him was a bad idea. He went for temporary—the right person for right now, and she wasn't cut out for that kind of life.

Jemima placed her mug carefully in the dishwasher. 'I don't do that kind of fun.'

'But you could,' Rachel said, her eyes watching her friend above the top of her mug.

'Don't be ridiculous. Look at me, Rachel.'

'I'm looking.'

'I lost my hip-bones some time around the age of twenty-one and I've got stretch marks you could use to design a board game. It's not going to happen. There's no way I'm going to get undressed in front of Miles.'

'But if he doesn't mind—'

'And how would we know that until it was too late? It's not going to happen, Rachel. Even with the light off,' she added as she saw her friend was about to speak. 'Hush. I think I hear them.'

The doorbell rang almost immediately and Jemima went to answer it.

'We're back,' Miles said, both hands on Ben's shoulders.

'We nearly capsized thirty-nine times! It was wicked.'

Jemima looked up into Miles's laughing blue eyes. 'Thirty-nine?'

'Takes skill, that.'

Whenever she was with Miles she wanted to smile. From behind her she heard running feet on the stairs and Sam hurled himself down the hallway. 'We've been painting the drawers in my bedroom.'

'Have you?' Miles said, reaching out and touching a strand of Jemima's hair. 'Let me guess. Blue.'

'Welkin Blue,' Jemima said. 'Left over from the bathroom. It's supposed to be the colour of a summer sky.'

Miles smiled down at her. 'It looks lovely.'

'Put her down, Miles,' Rachel said as she came to stand behind Jemima. 'There are people watching.'

'Just getting the paint out of her hair.'

'So I see.'

He calmly released Jemima's hair. 'One son returned without too much damage.'

Jemima didn't know how he managed to sound so cool. She felt hot and flustered. Knowing Rachel was watching them for the slightest sign of anything made her feel self-conscious and jumpy.

'Why don't you go through to the kitchen? Get yourself a coffee…or something,' she said, hardly daring to look Miles in the eye.

As soon as he had taken Ben through to the kitchen, Rachel leant forward and gave Jemima a light kiss on the cheek.

'What?'

Rachel grinned. 'Nothing. Nothing at all.'

CHAPTER TEN

MILES felt peculiar as he stood in the banqueting hall of Manningtree Castle. Really quite nervous—and he wasn't sure why that would be.

Candles flickered everywhere and the soft light created the kind of romantic setting that wouldn't have been out of place in a Hollywood version of *Robin Hood*. Flowers were studded through intricate swags of dark green foliage and atmospheric music wafted down from the gallery above.

It was incredible how everything had come together in such a short time. Rachel was going to have the wedding day of her dreams.

Miles reached into his pocket to check for the ring. It was still there. He must have checked for it at least half a dozen times in the last few minutes. He'd no idea why. This was his fourth outing as best man, so one would have thought he'd be icily calm and a real pillar of strength.

Instead he felt as if he was the one about to sign

his life away. Alistair, by contrast, looked completely cool. He'd been happily chatting to the eighty or so guests who'd assembled dutifully on dark red velvet chairs and he looked like a man who was thoroughly enjoying himself.

'Okay?' Alistair asked, looking across at him.

'Shouldn't that be my question?'

His friend merely smiled.

Miles glanced down at his watch. 'The girls are late.'

'That's their prerogative...' And then the music changed. 'Here we go.' Alistair turned to watch his bride walk over the polished floorboards towards him.

Miles swivelled round as the wedding guests all stood up as though they were one entity and he let his breath out in a steady stream. He was so nervous. And he didn't have the faintest idea why. Anyone would think *he* was the one getting married, instead of which...

He stopped thinking as Rachel came into view, but it wasn't the bride that had caused this cessation of all normal functions. It was Jemima. She looked...unbelievable. Beyond beautiful.

Miles smiled, feeling a strange mixture of pride and *care* for her. He knew how nervous Jemima had been about today. She didn't like being in the limelight, so this was always going to be difficult for her, but there was more to it than that.

She hadn't had to tell him how apprehensive she was about so many of her university friends coming to the wedding. For many, if not most, this was the first time they'd have seen her since her divorce. She had pride, his Jemima.

His.

That was how he thought of her now. Her worries had become his worries. He had this overwhelming need to make life better for her. Easier.

But, looking at her now, he couldn't imagine she'd ever need anything from him. She looked confident and breathtakingly lovely. Her rich copper hair had been left loose with the front sections twisted back and held in place by small white flowers. His eyes travelled lower to the simple column dress in an unusual russet brown and skimmed over the curves of her body. She'd told him she thought she looked ridiculous and that if there was a strong wind she might take off because of the sleeves. It was a description that didn't come close to doing justice to the fine gauze-like fabric, slashed from the elbow and elegantly falling to ground level.

She was stunning. And he felt a little in awe of her.

Jemima stepped forward and took Rachel's artfully natural bouquet and added it to her own. Miles wondered whether she'd had a chance yet to notice where Russell was sitting. He knew. His eyes had instinctively searched him out. Russell was sitting on the bride's side, six rows back.

Miles wondered, too, what Russell was thinking when he looked at Jemima. He felt nervously in his pocket for the ring as the short civil ceremony moved on. If memories crowded in on Jemima, surely they'd crowd in on her ex-husband too.

These were such new feelings and thoughts for him. In some kind of abstract way he'd always known that people came with a past. He'd known that specific incidents and even the general tenor of his childhood had shaped the man he was now. But…he'd not really been interested in any one other human being to want to know what had formed them.

Jemima was different. He was fascinated by her. She was reserved, self-effacing, witty, strong, beautiful… There were so many facets to her personality. She endlessly surprised him. In fact, she was like no other woman he'd spent time with. He loved being with her. Loved saying something that brought a burst of laughter. Loved making her blush.

And she never bored him. He reckoned she never would. Even after a lifetime. *Lifetime?*

Miles turned to look at Jemima, a little amazed by where his thoughts had taken him. She was so still. Her hands were clasped loosely on the bouquets she was holding and her eyes were focused on her friends. She hadn't looked at him.

Why hadn't she even glanced across in his direction?

'The ring?'

He'd almost missed his moment. Miles pulled it out of his pocket and handed it over. He'd been to scores of weddings over the past decade, but this was the first time he really listened to the promises the bride and groom were making. Understood what it *really* meant when Alistair slipped the gold band on Rachel's finger. Big promises, but it was actually quite beautiful.

Instinctively he glanced across to where Jemima was standing. She'd made those same promises to Russell. Had made them with the intention of keeping them. What was she thinking now? Was she reminded of her own wedding? Hurting?

Looking at her face, he thought not. She looked poised and strong. No one seeing the outward Jemima would guess she felt anything but pleasure at her friends' wedding. She was doing well, but he knew, because she'd let him glimpse beyond the capable façade, how much more complicated her emotions were.

His eyes wandered over to where Russell was sitting, presumably with Stefanie beside him. The man had made a poor trade, he thought. Why would any man choose a petulant-looking imitation blonde, who didn't seem to like his children, over Jemima?

But thank God he had, otherwise Miles knew he

would never have had the opportunity to get to know her, learn to love her…

Love her. He *loved* Jemima.

That should have come as a blinding revelation, but it didn't. Miles smiled slowly. *Of course,* he loved her. In the end it was as simple as walking from one room to another. He loved her.

And it felt terrific.

Suddenly 'for ever' didn't seem quite long enough. *And what did she feel about him?* Was it very arrogant to think she might love him too?

And then the ceremony was over. Miles reached out and took hold of Jemima's hand, threading it through his arm for the short walk across the banqueting hall. She looked up and smiled at him, the first time since she'd arrived.

'I'm glad that's over,' she whispered quietly. 'It went well, though, didn't it?'

'Now, as long as the marquee holds up we're on the home straight.'

She laughed. 'Oh, heck, and it'll be my fault if it doesn't. If ever I get married again I want to do nothing but turn up. This is too stressful.'

'I'll remember that.'

Jemima looked up at him and then away, but he'd caught the glimmer of something in her eyes. *What did it mean?* Then she moved away in order to help Rachel manage her long train as she walked down the stone spiral staircase.

The next three hours were strange. In many ways they were predictable. There were the endless photographs on the tulip lawn with the castle as a dramatic foil. Yet more had been taken on the Tudor bridge which spanned the dry moat. Then they moved seamlessly through a champagne reception and on into a wedding breakfast comprising six courses with a very twenty-first century feel.

What was strange was how much of a spectator he felt, despite being so involved in what was happening. He felt as if he was on the sidelines watching, waiting for his real life to start. And real life could only happen when he'd been able to speak to Jemima.

His speech as best man was everything Alistair and Rachel had hoped it would be, but it was Jemima's calm green eyes he looked at for approval. It was her slow smile that warmed him. He was anxious to know how she was doing, eager to be near her, but there was little possibility of that. Despite preferring to leave the limelight to others, Jemima was continually surrounded throughout the long afternoon.

In the end she found him.

'My feet ache,' she said, coming to stand beside him. She lifted up the hem of her dress and revealed matching shoes with viciously pointed toes.

He wondered how women could squeeze their feet into that tortuous shape and spared a moment to think how glad he was that male fashion hadn't evolved that way. 'That's twelfth century footwear for you.'

Jemima gave a gurgle of laughter. 'They'll be going soon. Have you done anything about Alistair's car?'

'It's all under control. I've organised rose petals to be put in the air vents and streamers practically everywhere else.'

He turned to look at her, loving the way her copper hair framed her beautiful face.

'I even managed to dissuade Alistair's young cousin from putting stones in the hub-caps and fish in place of the rose petals. Can you imagine how awful that would smell?'

'And how long it would have lasted,' Miles added. Then, 'Are you tired?'

'Shattered. My face aches from continually smiling and I'm longing for a cup of tea.'

Miles laughed and reached out for her hand. 'Come and find five minutes quiet. They won't leave for a good half an hour yet.'

She hesitated, he thought, but then she let him lead her away from the hubbub of noise and along by the lake. 'It is beautiful here,' Jemima remarked, looking out across the lake. 'I would never have changed my wedding venue so late in the day, but

I can see why Rachel felt she had to do it. There's something rather special about standing where kings and queens have been entertained.'

Miles moved to stand beside her. He had to tell her what he was feeling. And he had to tell her now. It wouldn't wait.

There was a moment's silence and then he said, 'I love you.' His voice was quiet and his eyes were focused far in the distance.

He felt her turn to look at him and he moved so that he could see her face. He noticed the small pulse in her neck and her wide eyes. His smile twisted at her surprise.

'I love you.' Miles swallowed, searching for the words that would convey to her exactly how far he'd travelled in the past three months. 'I didn't know... I haven't ever felt...'

Words never failed him. But now, when they really mattered, he couldn't find them. There was so much he wanted her to understand. He pulled an agitated hand through his hair. 'I love you,' he repeated, reaching for her hands and holding her listless fingers in his firm grasp.

'You love me?'

'And I want you to marry me. I want for ever.'

He'd said it. The words he'd thought he'd never say to anyone. He wanted a future with Jemima as his wife more than he wanted his freedom. He knew with complete certainty that she was the woman he wanted to spend the rest of his life with. That if she said no his life would always be a pale imitation of what it could have been with her beside him.

He looked into Jemima's face, searching for some reaction other than surprise. He found it in the soft shimmer of tears that covered her green eyes.

'Miles, I—I can't.'

His mouth moved soundlessly and his body felt cold.

Jemima pulled her hands away and covered her trembling mouth. 'I'm so sorry, Miles.'

'Why?'

She shook her head as though she didn't want to explain, but then the words were drawn from her anyway. 'I never thought…' Jemima moved nearer. 'You said you didn't believe in marriage,' she said, almost accusing.

'I know. I didn't.' His eyes willed her to understand, to feel how much he loved her. Would always love her. 'I've never felt like this before. I've never been in love, so it took me a while to understand what I was feeling. And…then, today, I listened to the promises Alistair and Rachel were making and…I want that. I want to know you're going to walk the rest of your life beside me, loving me, supporting me.'

Jemima's hand felt for a coil of her hair and

twisted it round her finger. Her green eyes were full of fear and pain. 'When I married Russell I really believed it would be for ever. I thought he was a steady kind of man who really loved me.'

Miles went to speak, but she stopped him.

'You…you're not safe enough for me. I've got two boys—'

'I know, I—'

'And I'm not brave enough. I can't risk them being hurt…and I can't risk being hurt myself. I'd always be wondering why you were with me. Whether you'd met someone you found more attractive, more amusing, more… Well, more.'

Miles felt as though something had reached deep inside him and had taken hold of his heart and was squeezing it with long, tenacious fingers. 'Jemima, I love you.'

He watched with an acute kind of pain the moisture well up in her eyes and fall in soft tears down her cheeks. Miles went to move, but she held him off. 'I'm so sorry. Really s-sorry.'

And then she walked away, back along the lakeside path. Miles remained still for a moment, too wounded to move. Loving, he realised, came at a cost. Until this moment his understanding of rejection had been entirely cerebral, but if Jemima had experienced a fraction of the pain he felt now…

He would wait for her, he thought with quiet determination. Slowly he would win her round, make her love him enough to be prepared to risk anything.

'What's happened?' Rachel asked, looking anxiously at Jemima's tear-stained face.

'Nothing. I'm sorry. It's nothing.'

'Is it Russell?'

Jemima shook her head.

Rachel looked past her and saw Miles coming out of the woods. 'Miles?'

'It's nothing, really,' Jemima said, summoning up a brave smile. 'I'm being ridiculous. Are you and Alistair about to leave?'

'We were,' she said, still looking concerned. 'Alistair was going to look for Miles and then we were going back to the cottage to get changed. But if you're upset we can—'

Jemima reached out to hug her friend. 'I really hope you'll both be very happy. I'm just feeling emotional. It's nothing. It's been a very emotional day,' she said, pulling back and smiling bravely.

It was amazing to Jemima that Rachel believed her. Even more amazing that her over-bright smile appeared to fool everyone else as well.

Inside she was falling apart, piece by piece. All she wanted was solitude where she could begin to unpack the emotions that were building inside her. *Miles loved her.* If she hadn't known that was an impossibility she might have been more prepared. But that he loved her enough to *marry* her… There was no amount of preparation that would have made her ready to hear that.

It was a fairytale. It was the knight on horseback climbing up the tower to rescue his princess. Or the foreign prince waking his love with a kiss. It was everything she'd ever dreamed of…just there within her reach. If she only had the courage to reach out and take hold of it…

As soon as she'd waved Alistair and Rachel away, Jemima quietly slipped back into the woodland. Perhaps if she hadn't been so sure of Russell she might feel braver now. But…

She had been sure of him. She'd skipped through her wedding day with the confidence of someone who knew she'd be happy for the rest of her life.

And yet… It had all come down to a rainy Sunday afternoon when she'd been told she'd become boring. That the man she believed loved her no longer found her physically attractive…

'Jemima.'

She turned to see Russell standing there, almost as though he'd been conjured up by her thoughts.

'May I…talk to you?'

Jemima felt too empty to care whether he stayed or whether he went. He probably wanted to ask if he could have the boys longer over the summer. No doubt his mother wanted them to visit her in Devon.

Russell must have taken her silence for tacit agreement because he sat down beside her. He cleared his throat with a dry cough. 'You look lovely.'

She looked across at him, surprised. 'Thank you.'

Russell looked down at his hands and cleared his throat again. He seemed tense and nervous. Jemima waited for what would come next.

'Stefanie…'

She was too tired, too heart-sore to sit here while Russell talked about Stefanie. She didn't *care* any more what they did. She just wished she didn't have to see them or think about them.

Again that irritating dry cough. 'Stefanie is pregnant.'

Jemima turned to look at him. 'Pregnant?'

'Four months.' Russell nodded. 'Not planned.'

'Oh.' What else could she say? It didn't seem quite appropriate to say 'congratulations'. She didn't quite know why he thought he ought to tell her. It was nothing to do with her any more…

Except, of course, that the baby would be a half-brother or sister to Ben and Sam. Even so, she thought it was his responsibility to tell them the news. Ben would hate it. Sam would probably be pleased.

'I…er…'

Jemima looked at him curiously.

'Are you and Miles…?'

She found that she was getting impatient with this whole conversation. She had so much else to think about. It was none of Russell's business whether she and Miles were or weren't. He could hardly expect they'd be able to sit companionably side by side discussing their respective love lives.

'I'm sorry, I…' He stood up restlessly and then sat down beside her again. 'I hated it when you got pregnant with Sam,' he said suddenly.

Jemima couldn't quite believe what she was hearing.

'I love him now. Of course I do. But I found the whole pregnancy difficult. You know, the antenatal classes, the house being full of baby things. It was worse with Sam because I knew what was coming. And you were always so tired—'

Jemima cut him off. 'I don't think I need to hear this,' she said, standing up.

'Jemma.' His voice stopped her. 'If I could do things differently, I would.'

Jemima turned and her dress swooshed on the path.

Russell's eyes looked up bleakly. 'I've made a mess of everything, haven't I? I suppose there's no way…no way back…?'

Any way back? To her?

'Is there?'

No. There was no way back. Jemima moved to sit beside him. It was strange how 'little' he seemed to her now. Not the handsome, strong man she'd thought she'd married, but a little boy. Confused, frightened by responsibility. She was sad for him.

She reached out and touched his hand. 'You're with Stefanie now. That's the choice you made.'

A muscle flicked in his cheek. 'I suppose…'

'She's not like you, Jemima. I—' he smiled sadly and then found the word he was searching for '—miss you. Does that sound strange?'

Jemima wasn't sure whether it did or didn't. In a way, she understood. She missed the dream she'd had. As she looked at Russell, she realised that she'd spent nearly three years of her life mourning the loss of that far more than the man himself.

'We had some good years.'

'Yes.'

She felt almost as if she was talking to one of her sons rather than the man she'd once thought she'd spend her life loving. 'And we share two fantastic boys. But we have different futures ahead of us now.'

'You don't love me?'

'No. No, I don't.' And she really didn't. Searching inside herself, there was no sense of regret. When she looked at Russell she felt…nothing.

'Miles is a lucky man,' Russell said, putting his

arms around her and holding her. It seemed rude to push him away, so Jemima stayed still.

Vaguely she heard the sound of footsteps and then Miles's voice sliced through the air. 'I'm sorry. I...'

'Miles!' Jemima pulled away from Russell and looked up into Miles's eyes. They were bleak, as though his soul had been ripped out of him. For a moment she didn't understand the expression on his face and then she felt as though she'd been torpedoed. Miles thought... He thought...

'I didn't realise Russell was with you,' he said with quiet dignity. 'I'm sorry.' Then he turned to walk away without waiting for her to say anything.

Oh, God, please, no.

Jemima sat, stunned. She'd never heard such a raw edge of pain in anyone's voice. Not even hers. Her limbs were slow to respond. She wasn't sure what she ought to do now. She only knew that Miles was hurting—and she had to find him.

'Russell, I'm going to have to go,' she said, standing up. 'I'll talk to you about the boys next week, but I've got to go...'

She trailed off and walked briskly down the woodland path. She came out on to the tulip lawn and looked around her. She couldn't see him anywhere. She slipped off her high-heeled shoes and almost ran across the soft grass.

'Jemima.' Alistair's second cousin stopped her.

'I'm looking for Miles. Have you seen him?'

'No. Oh, yes, he was going towards the marquee.'

It was the start of a horrible fifteen minutes. Miles seemed to have vanished. He wasn't in the marquee or even back at the castle. It was almost as though aliens had landed and he'd been plucked from the earth.

Jemima stood listlessly looking at the Tudor bridge, finally accepting that he'd gone. Home? Possibly. Most of the guests had either left or were on the point of leaving.

He was hurting. It was almost unbelievable that she could have the power to hurt a man like Miles. *She had that power because he loved her*—loved *her*—and in her fear she'd thrown that love back in his face. Had hurt him. She picked up the front of her dress and walked purposefully towards her hired car. He loved her.

And she loved him. Not like she'd loved Russell. That had been…different somehow. Maybe it was because they'd been so much younger, but…

This felt scarier. She'd thought her fear was because she was too scared to risk her heart on another relationship, but actually it was because she knew she wouldn't survive Miles falling out of love with her.

But then she'd seen the pain in Miles's eyes as he'd seen Russell holding her. It had changed everything. Every thought in her body was that she needed to get to him, talk to him…

The journey back to London seemed to take for ever. She didn't even have a very clear idea of what she intended to do when she got there. The traffic slowed to a snail's pace as she reached the outskirts of town and she felt more impatient than she'd ever done before.

She didn't even think about how strange she must look still dressed in her bridesmaid's dress when she stopped for petrol. It was as though she was running on pure adrenaline.

And all the time she was planning what she should do. She could phone him, but she didn't think she could say what she wanted to without being able to see his face. She had to see him. And it had to be tonight.

Although she'd never been to his house, she had his address on a piece of paper tucked inside the front pocket of her handbag. It meant she had to drive to Harrow first.

What if he wasn't at home? Well, if he wasn't she'd have to phone him then. But only if he wasn't home.

'Jemima!' her mum exclaimed, looking up as she ran through the lounge. 'I didn't expect you back yet.'

'I know. I…' Her fingers fumbled with the front clasp of her handbag and she pulled out the piece of paper. 'Are the boys okay?'

'They're fine. Fast asleep.'

'Mum, I've just made the most terrible mistake. I…' Her voice cracked and her mum smiled.

'Miles?' she said gently.

'I've got to go and find him.'

'Good idea.' Her mum settled back into her armchair. 'I'll stay with the boys, so don't hurry back.'

In a whirl of russet fabric, Jemima tore out of the house. She was so focused on what she was doing that she didn't notice that she drove up a bus lane and twice cut up the same black cab.

It was only when she approached Miles's house that she felt any sense of nervousness. She was used to seeing him in her own home, even against the stylish backdrop of Kingsley and Bressington, but this was money. Money as Verity lived it. It felt a little strange.

She parked the car and managed to find change for the meter. His house was tucked away in a small mews—double-fronted with its own garage. She remembered now that he'd told her he'd bought it because it had a place to keep his precious car.

Jemima picked up the hem of her dress and walked towards the blue front door. *She could do this. She really could.* Her heart was pounding but she was filled with an uncharacteristic exuberance.

Without giving herself time to think any more about what she was going to say, or what Miles might say to her, Jemima pushed the bell. Then she waited, her ears straining to hear the sound of his footsteps coming to answer the door.

There was silence. Perhaps he'd decided not to come home. Perhaps…

And then the door opened.

He looked dreadful. He'd changed from his wedding clothes and he looked…broken. She'd never imagined Miles could look like that.

She wasn't sure how to begin to explain why she was here. It had seemed so simple back in Kent. She loved *him*, not Russell, and she wanted him to know that. Russell was her past, not her future.

Miles didn't ask her in. He seemed confused that she was there, braced to be hurt. She understood how that felt.

Jemima moistened her lips. 'I…'

'Yes?'

'I came to tell you… I…' She broke off again and cursed herself inwardly for not having worked out exactly what she was going to say.

'Yes?'

'I came to tell you I'm sorry. That I…'

Miles stepped back into his house as though she'd hit him. He seemed to expect that she'd follow, so she did, shutting the door behind her.

She'd never felt so nervous in her entire life. What if Miles had only asked her to marry him as a momentary impulse?

But what if he was hurting?

Jemima moistened her lips. 'Miles.'

He'd picked up a whisky tumbler and took a sip. 'Can I get you anything? Wine? Tea? Coffee?'

It was difficult to speak to him when he was like this. Everything was making it seem harder to say what she needed to, even their being in his starkly beautiful home rather than somewhere familiar to her.

'Miles.' She moistened her lips again. 'I came to tell you—'

'That you're taking Russell back?' His voice was thick with pain and Jemima lost her English reserve.

'No.' She shook her head. 'No, I came to tell you that I love *you*.'

It was as though something snapped inside him. She heard the sound of his glass being put down roughly on the table and then she felt his hands tenderly cradling her face.

'Say that again,' he instructed, looking deep into her eyes.

It was easier this time. Her smile was tremulous. 'I love you. And—'

But she didn't get a chance to finish what she was saying because he was kissing her with a desperation that was incredibly erotic. His voice was husky as he said her name and Jemima let her hands snake up to bury themselves deep in his dark hair.

It was going to be all right. Not just all right—it was going to be incredible. She felt tears of relief start in her eyes.

'I thought I'd lost you.'

Jemima didn't pretend to misunderstand. 'To Russell? No. I love you.'

She heard the soft groan he made at the back of his throat and then he was kissing her again. His mouth was warm and tasted of whisky and her body responded as though it were liquid heat. She'd never experienced anything so instantaneous. So…mindblowingly sexy.

There would be time later, much later, to tell him about Russell's new baby. All about their conversation in the wood. For now it was enough that Miles was holding her as though he'd never let her go. More than enough.

Miles pulled back and stroked his thumbs gently over her tear-stained cheeks. 'You taste of salt.'

'You taste of whisky.'

He smiled then, that twisting sexy smile that made her feel light-headed. 'I was depressed.'

'That's a very bad reason for drinking whisky. You need taking in hand.'

'I know.'

Jemima took a deep breath and looked into his glinting blue eyes. 'Will you marry me?'

Slowly, very slowly, Miles traced his thumb across her lips, his face inexpressibly tender.

'You're asking me to marry you?' he said, his voice thick with wonder.

Her stomach was churning with a mixture of nervousness and excitement. 'Will you?'

'Try stopping me.'

EPILOGUE

JEMIMA stood outside the church and experienced a moment of intense panic at the enormity of what she was doing. Her heart started to beat erratically and her legs felt like blancmange. *She couldn't do this*.

What if Miles changed his mind five years down the track? What if he woke up one morning and realised he didn't love her any more? What if he'd already realised he was making a terrible mistake and was standing at the front of the church now wishing he wasn't?

'Ready?' Rachel asked, smoothing one wayward curl back off Jemima's forehead.

'I'm scared.'

Her friend looked at her and then asked gently, 'Is that nervous scared, or scared scared?'

Jemima's hands started to tremble. 'I'm scared this is the wrong thing.'

'For you, or for him?' Rachel asked sagely.

Then, in spite of the hand-tied bouquet of white roses, she took hold of Jemima's cold hands. 'Look at me, Jemima.'

Slowly Jemima brought her frightened eyes away from the arched church door and looked into Rachel's unusually calm and sensible ones.

'This is *Miles* you're marrying. There's nothing to be scared about.'

I'm marrying Miles. Jemima repeated Rachel's words in her head and felt the fear recede as quickly as it had come. *Miles.*

'I've seen you make some daft decisions. Not many, but some,' Rachel said with a smile. 'This isn't one of them.'

No, it wasn't. It absolutely wasn't.

Rachel released her fingers and Jemima looked down at the engagement ring Miles had chosen for her, but it wasn't the beauty of the princess cut diamond she saw. She saw instead the amazing man who'd given it to her.

And she saw the expression in his eyes when he'd presented it to her. They'd been standing in a capsule on the London Eye on a balmy late August evening, the city lights dramatic in the night sky.

It had been one of those golden moments, the kind you knew you'd remember until the day you died. He'd pulled the small velvet box from his pocket and had told her he loved her, the woman she was and the woman she'd become.

She'd been a little scared that day. Part of her had been worried that if she allowed herself to be too happy it would hurt more when it was snatched away. And Miles had known that, had understood why.

Jemima passed Rachel her simple bouquet to hold and twisted her engagement ring off her finger, transferring it to her right hand for the ceremony.

There'd been moments during their engagement when that fear had risen to the surface. Days when she'd been so sure Miles would look at her and realise she wasn't what he wanted.

Like the day when Sam had ridden his bike slap bang into his prized Bristol 407 and made a horrible scratch along the right passenger door. Jemima smiled wryly. *She'd been certain Miles would leave her then*.

Then there was the time when he'd been left kicking his heels outside Ben's classroom because Russell had unexpectedly been able to make parents' evening after all. *She'd been terrified he'd leave her then*.

Jemima took back her bouquet from Rachel and smiled. 'I'm marrying Miles.'

'And he loves you,' Rachel said, adjusting the single white rose amidst the copper curls. 'Very much. Your sad times are all behind you.'

No more sad times. It was something Jemima thought of all the way down the aisle. Such a short distance and yet it felt so far.

She was vaguely aware of the music that heralded her entrance and the faces of close friends and family. Her mother was a blur of soft dove-grey and Hermione a more noticeable figure in burgundy, but mostly she saw Miles waiting for her, Ben beside him.

Miles turned to watch her. Tall, dark, handsome…actually, very handsome…and *hers*. Rachel was wrong. There would be sad times. But there'd also be happy times, exciting times…

And there'd be Miles.

Hers. *For better, for worse. In sickness and in health. Forsaking all others.*

And she believed him. Absolutely.

It meant that when Miles promised to love her until she died she knew he'd keep that promise, whatever the future held for them. It was the time for *doubting* that was over.

And when Ben, as best man, solemnly passed over the gold band and Miles slid it on her finger, Jemima felt a sense of peace.

'…*pronounce you man and wife. You may kiss your bride.*'

Jemima looked up into his blue eyes and she knew he meant it when he said softly, 'I love you, Mrs Kingsley.'

Her own eyes twinkled up at him. 'Then you'd better kiss me.'

His hands cradled her face and he did just that,

his lips saying more than the words of the church service. Then he reached down and touched Ben on the head. A simple gesture, but it was something Jemima knew she'd never forget.

Just as she wouldn't forget the sight of the traditionally painted Gypsy caravan pulled by one horse as it came round the corner towards the church.

She looked up at her new husband, a question in her eyes.

'You said different,' he said, reaching down to hold her hand. 'Good idea?'

It was strange how close laughter and tears were, because Jemima suddenly felt as if she wanted to cry. 'Brilliant idea.'

'No ghosts, then?'

She shook her head. 'No ghosts.'

Then Miles smiled and it came as a blinding revelation to her that he'd been worried there might be. She reached up and touched his face. 'I love you.'

'Just me,' he said with mock severity. 'No one else.'

Jemima shook her head and held up her left hand. 'I promised.'

His eyes took on their customary glint. 'I'll hold you to that,' he said, leading her towards the Gypsy caravan that would take them to their reception. 'I love you, too. And I really love your "something blue". Very sexy. Are brides supposed to be sexy?'

Jemima smoothed out the ice-blue silk of the elegant but simple dress she'd chosen to be married in. Then she looked up, a mischievous twinkle in her own eyes. 'Just wait till you see what I'm wearing that's white,' she said, teasing. 'I think you're really going to love that.'

First comes love, then comes marriage...

That was Gracie's plan, anyway, at the ripe old age of fourteen. She loved eighteen-year-old heart throb Riley with a legendary desperation. Even now that she's all grown up, the locals in her sleepy town won't let her forget her youthful crush.

...but it's not as easy as it looks.
And now she's face-to-face with Riley at every turn. The one-time bad boy has come back seeking respectability – but the sparks that fly between them are anything but respectable! Gracie's determined to keep her distance, but when someone sets out to ruin both their reputations, the two discover that first love sometimes is better the second time around.

On sale 1st September 2006

Can you tell from first impressions whether someone could become your closest friend?

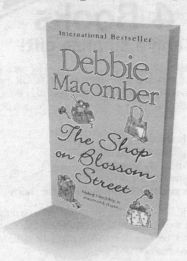

Lydia, Jacqueline, Carol and Alix are four very different women, each facing their own problems in life. When they are thrown together by the hands of fate, none of them could ever guess how close they would become or where their friendship would lead them.

A heartfelt, emotional tale of friendship and problems shared from a multi-million copy bestselling author.

On sale 18th August 2006

FREE!

4 Books
and a surprise gift!

We would like to take this opportunity to thank you for reading this Mills & Boon® book by offering you the chance to take FOUR more specially selected titles from the Romance series absolutely FREE! We're also making this offer to introduce you to the benefits of the Mills & Boon® Reader Service™—

★ **FREE home delivery**
★ **FREE gifts and competitions**
★ **FREE monthly Newsletter**
★ **Exclusive Reader Service offers**
★ **Books available before they're in the shops**

Accepting these FREE books and gift places you under no obligation to buy, you may cancel at any time, even after receiving your free shipment. Simply complete your details below and return the entire page to the address below. You don't even need a stamp!

YES! Please send me 4 free Romance books and a surprise gift. I understand that unless you hear from me, I will receive 6 superb new titles every month for just £2.80 each, postage and packing free. I am under no obligation to purchase any books and may cancel my subscription at any time. The free books and gift will be mine to keep in any case.

N6ZEF

Ms/Mrs/Miss/Mr ....Initials................................
                                                                BLOCK CAPITALS PLEASE
Surname ....
Address...

....
....Postcode ....

Send this whole page to:
UK: FREEPOST CN81, Croydon, CR9 3WZ